# All I Want For Christmas Is An Alpha

BY

MONI BOYCE

LOVE SNACKS
PUBLISHING

# All I Want For Christmas Is An Alpha

# PROLOGUE

## 16 Years Ago

"How did you find me?" Adrenaline coursed through my veins.

I thought I'd been careful. I'm always careful. How had she tracked me from the school? Part of me had known that one day someone would, but I hadn't expected it to be her.

She didn't answer me right away. She just looked around the tent, her eyes taking in my sleeping bag, plastic water jug, small stash of food, meager clothing and a few other odds and ends. Under her scrutiny, I felt shame and anger at my situation. I tried to swallow it down. My face was hot, and my hands were curled into tight angry fists. Considering I'd been bullying her for the last month, taking whatever I could from her, I expected her to make fun of me, to laugh, tell me she was going to tell everyone at school.

When her warm brown eyes landed back on me, there was no pity there or malice.

"Are you hungry?"

In my confusion, my mouth opened and closed, but no words came out. That's not what I'd been expecting from her.

Instantly, I was on the defensive. What was she playing at? "Is this some sort of trick?" My eyes narrowed in suspicion, and I continued to stare at her.

"No, you idiot. I'm asking if you're hungry. It's not a joke or a prank."

Where was that attitude when I'd been taking her lunch money every day? We stared at each other.

Finally, I answered. "I could eat."

My stomach chose that moment to give a loud grumble, like it needed to confirm what I'd said.

"Well c'mon then." She turned on her heel.

It took a second, but I followed her. When we ended up at her house, I almost turned around and left. Adults were only trouble.

"Where are you going?"

"I'm leaving."

"Why? I thought you said you were hungry?" Her face was twisted up in puzzlement.

"You're going to tell your parents I don't have a home and then they'll call the cops or someone who'll throw me in foster care. Thanks, but no thanks. I can take care of myself." I turned and walked away.

"Cooper... wait."

She ran up and came to stand in front of me. "I won't say anything if you don't want me to, but you have to eat right?"

I looked at the ground, and then back at her. "Yeah."

"Okay then. Stay for dinner." She turned back towards her house.

I hadn't started following her yet. "What are you going to tell your mom and dad when they ask about me?"

I came up beside her and waited.

"I'll just tell them that you came over for us to work on a project and I invited you to stay for dinner."

Disbelief was etched into my face when I looked at her. "You'd lie to your parents for me?"

For a minute, she looked away, thinking about what I'd just said. Exactly what I thought. I knew she was about to say I was right, and she couldn't lie to them.

Suddenly, her face lit up in a grin, like she'd just discovered money in her pocket.

"It won't be lying if I'm keeping my friend's secret."

When she said the word friend, a funny feeling crept through my body. "We're friends?"

"If you want to be." She tried to hide how much she hoped I said yes.

This was a first for me. No one had ever wanted to be my friend before. I tried to

act as nonchalant as she had about it. "I guess I'm okay with that."

We began to walk towards her house.

I slung my arm across her shoulders. "By the way, if we're friends now. You can call me Coop."

She grinned. "Okay."

"You have any nicknames?"

Macy shook her head.

I grinned showing all of my teeth. "Now you do. I'm going to call you Mace... Mace in your face." I kind of sing-songed the last part.

She'd started out with an excited look on her face. When I added that last part, she shook her head vehemently. I laughed. "Okay, just Mace."

# CHAPTER 1

## Cooper

**Present Day**

The way this chick was using her tongue and mouth had my eyes rolling back in my head. It felt incredible. When I put my hand in her hair, she made the most delicious purr with her mouth that vibrated around my dick and nearly made me come. I groaned at the exquisite pleasure she was torturing me with. Gripping her hair, I pulled it away from her face so I could watch her deep throat my...

She lifted up her head and looked at me.

"What the fuck?" My eyes opened wide in shock and I sat up quickly. I took a ragged breath and ran my hand through my hair. "Macy?" Why was my best friend, giving me head in my dream?

That was not the first dream I'd had about Macy. In the last month, I'd been dreaming of her off and on, but this was the first time we'd been having any type of sex. The other dreams were still equally as strange. In one, she'd been wearing a white dress. Yes, that type of white dress. This was getting too weird. I wasn't sure what to make of all of this. Honestly, I didn't want to examine any of it too closely.

Unfortunately, my brain seemed to have other plans. The rest of the morning, while I got ready for my day, I couldn't stop pondering why she was in my dreams: while I showered, drunk my coffee, on the way to work. The thought was fixated in my brain.

"Morning, Mr. Brayden." Lou, the security guard, greeted me before I got on the elevator.

"Hey Lou." I said absently.

Instrumental Christmas music played in the background on my ride up to our floor. When the elevator doors opened, I stepped into our lobby which had been made to look like a very chic winter wonderland. The employees loved going all out with the decorations, but I still wanted it to look classy. We catered to a high-end clientele. I didn't want it looking like the eyesore of the Griswold's front lawn.

I made it to my office and shut the door. Even though we would soon be shut down for the holidays, I still had one major deal on a sweet piece of commercial real estate I was hoping to close. After taking off my coat and hanging it up, I grabbed the contract from my briefcase and sat at my desk.

My cell phone rang. When I saw it was Macy calling, I let it go to voicemail. I was still too shaken from my dream this morning to talk to her. Once she left a message, I played it.

"I didn't want to talk to you over voicemail about this, but I would really appreciate it if you would go with me to Jennifer's wedding." There was a pause. "Patrick is going to be there, and I don't want to go alone. Call me back, Coop."

The anxious, desperate tone in Macy's voice made me grind my teeth. I hung up the phone without deleting her message. Why did she care that her asshole ex-boyfriend was going to be at the wedding? I'd never liked Patrick. He was all wrong for her. Too serious and straightlaced. Macy could do better. In the past, I'd never cared about who Macy dated. As long as the guy never laid a hand on her, I never laid a hand on them. This was different. I wasn't sure I wanted to examine why I was suddenly concerned with her feelings for her ex.

We were supposed to meet for dinner tonight, and I planned on telling her she should go to the wedding alone. Girl power and all that shit.

After that I managed to work for a few hours uninterrupted, before someone knocked on my office door. I checked my watch. Lunchtime.

Yesterday, I'd agreed to let Gladys, my assistant, take a long lunch to finish up her Christmas shopping, so I was fielding my own calls and unfortunately having to deal with people interrupting my work, people she would usually turn away.

I huffed. "Come in."

My partner, Martin Camden walked in. "How's it going with the contract for the Mercer project, Coop?" He perched on the edge of my desk, pissing me off.

"Don't sit on my desk."

Martin laughed and stood. He walked around my office, picking up decorative items and putting them back down while he spoke. "With the holidays coming up, I know we're looking to close this deal before the new year."

*Tell me something I don't know, Captain Obvious.*

His circuit around the room led him to the shelf that housed my photos. Martin picked one up. "There are a lot of pictures here of you and your girlfriend, Macy." He gestured towards the myriad of photographs that crowded the shelf.

Getting up from my desk, I crossed towards him and took the picture out of his hand. "How many times do I have to tell you, Mace is my friend." I placed the picture of Macy and I on vacation back on the shelf. "She's not my girlfriend." I didn't bother hiding the irritation in my voice.

Some people formed partnerships with friends. Martin and I had formed Brayden/Camden and Associates Brokerage Firm, because it was a good business strategy. We both excelled at what we did. I wasn't exactly friendly with the guy. In fact, he annoyed me, which is why Gladys usually ran interference. I think he purposely waited until she wasn't at her desk to knock on my door.

"Was there something else you needed besides distracting me and annoying the shit out of me?" I went back to my desk and sat.

Martin stuffed his hands into the pockets of his slacks and followed me over to my desk. He stood in front of it, peering down at the document I'd been perusing before he came in my office being a pain. "Nope..." He rocked back on his heels. "I don't have to remind you how important closing this deal is."

My gaze flicked up to meet his. "No." I delivered the one-word response in a deadpan voice. For several seconds, we just stared at each other.

"Okay then... I'll leave you to it."

Martin turned and walked away.

"Close the door on your way out."

I went back to outlining the document. Yes, I could do the same thing on my computer, but I was kind of old school when it came to handling contracts. I liked to print them out and mark them up with red pen.

It was hard concentrating, because my mind was still stuck on what Martin had said about Macy being my girlfriend. People had been mistaking us for a couple for as long as I could remember, so I wasn't sure why it seemed to bother me now. Maybe, it was the dream, or I was just irritated because it was Martin. Yep, that's what it was. Martin.

When I tried to go back to my work, I found myself looking at the picture of Macy and I that sat on my desk. Even when I had girlfriends their pictures never made it into my office to be prominently displayed.

The picture of the two of us had been taken a couple years ago during a holiday celebration at her parents' house. She'd always just been Mace to me, the girl I'd known since we were thirteen. Don't get me wrong, Mace was a beautiful woman. Even now, as I peered at her in the picture, I could appreciate her beauty. I'm a man.

Macy's beautiful, flawless brown skin had a warm undertone that made her look like she was being lit from within by the sun. Her mane of dark, black natural hair billowed out around her in soft waves. Macy was pretty tall for a woman. I was six foot one, and she was only a few inches shorter than me.

She had the best smile. It lit up her whole face when she was happy. Normally, I didn't notice her body. Okay, that was a lie. I'd noticed Macy's body since we were teenagers. How could I not? She had an athletic, curvy build that...

I shook my head, trying to dislodge these thoughts. *Stop thinking about your best friend like that.*

After giving the photo one final look, I went back to my work.

It was nothing. The dream was just a dream. Nothing was going to change... I just wish I believed that.

# CHAPTER 2

## Macy


The twinkling lights that decorated Rush Street and Nat King Cole singing about chestnuts roasting on an open fire should have had me in a festive mood, but I hadn't been feeling the holiday spirit ever since Jennifer told me Patrick was coming to the wedding with a plus one. He certainly wasn't bringing his brother, mother or some other family member or platonic friend. I wondered what my replacement looked like. Did she have bigger boobs? Was she shorter and more petite?

We'd broken up a couple months ago, or should I say he broke up with me, using the lame, 'It's not you, it's me,' cliché. It was completely unexpected. I thought things were going well between us.

Unfortunately, I still cared about him. I couldn't show up alone to my friend's wedding. I had to show Patrick what he was missing, which is why I had to convince Coop to not only attend the wedding, but to go as my boyfriend.

While I maneuvered my car into the parking space, my mind continued to wonder who would be accompanying my ex to the wedding. Then I wondered why Coop hadn't returned my call this afternoon. Had he even listened to my message?

Before I could exit the car, my cell phone rang. When I saw the number, I almost didn't answer it. It was one of my needy clients. I sighed and answered. "Hi, Mr. Farber. You know it's after hours." Listening as he prattled on about what we'd already discussed earlier.

"I told you this afternoon, everything looks good for the audit. You have nothing to worry about. Now any other questions, please call during business hours tomorrow." As a CPA with my own accounting firm, I dealt with clients all year long. Certain times of year, they definitely became a bit more needy and neurotic.

I got out of the car and walked towards the elevator. The sting of the crisp, cold air had me pulling the collar of my coat tighter to keep out the chill. I loved Chicago, but winters here could be brutal.

Thankfully, the elevator wasn't crowded. My head was still a mess on my trek to the restaurant. It felt good to step inside the cozy warmth of the steakhouse.

I let the maître d take my coat while I looked around the room for Coop. His golden blonde head was bent over his phone. He furiously tapped on the keyboard sending a text or email.

"Hey, sorry I'm late." I dropped into my seat, but he didn't look up.

"Remember the rule... no phones at the dinner table unless it's an emergency."

"I thought that only applied at your mother's house." He continued to type away on his phone without looking up at me.

"C'mon Coop. You know that rule applies when we have dinner as well."

"You and your rules." He groused, but his hands slowed on the keys. He hit send and then turned his cell phone face down on the table. "Happy?"

I ignored his whining. "How come you didn't answer my call this morning?" I put my napkin in my lap and signaled the waiter.

"I was busy with things at the office."

Coop didn't look me in the eye when he answered, which was unlike him. Before I could ask him anything else, the waiter appeared.

"Would you like to hear tonight's specials?" The waiter looked between us.

"No, we know what we want." There Coop was grumbling again. Something was up.

He was right. Neither of us had bothered to open the menus sitting in front of us. We came here often enough, and both of us always ordered the same thing.

"I'll have the salmon with the creamed spinach and the potatoes au gratin. Also, bring me a martini." I sat back in my seat and watched Coop while he ordered.

"Ribeye, rare. Green beans and a baked potato. Whiskey neat." He grabbed both of our menus from the table and handed them to the waiter.

While Coop glanced around the crowded room, I was struck by how attractive he was. Not that I wasn't made aware of it every time we were together. Whenever I was out with him, it didn't go unnoticed how many women did a double-take or tried to get his attention. Some were so taken by him that they didn't even notice me. Others would size me up, wondering if I was his wife, girlfriend, competition. The charisma he exuded filled the room. Women wanted to be with him, and men wanted to be associated with him.

Often his short, blonde hair was tousled like he'd been running his fingers through it most of the day. All year long his skin maintained a deep tan that looked like he'd been laying out at the beach all day. I knew he didn't fake and bake. We'd been friends since middle school and often went on vacation together, so I'd seen him practically naked many times. Coop's body was a sculpted masterpiece. He was faithful to his workouts and it showed. He was also one of the few guys I could wear heels with, and he wasn't intimidated by my height.

Of course, I found him attractive, but we'd been friends for so long. There was a brief time in college when I considered dating him, but I didn't want to lose our friendship.

"What's up?" Even though I was eager to talk about my problem, I wanted to make sure he was okay.

"Hmm?" He finally looked at me. It was like he was coming out of some sort of stupor.

Coop was usually very attentive, so it was odd that he seemed so distracted. "You had this look on your face a minute ago."

"Nothing. Just a little preoccupied with closing this deal... I did listen to your message."

He was changing the subject. We didn't have secrets from each other, but I decided to let it go for now.

"I couldn't believe that Jennifer sent him an invite. I know she said it's because he's Kai's friend, but... so will you go with me?"

Coop ran his hand through his hair. "What do you feel you have to prove to this jackass? What happened to being Miss Independent Woman?"

I snorted. "Very funny. I can still be an independent woman and want to have a date when I attend my friend's wedding."

"If you just need a date hire someone. I can see if Eddie's available. He likes a free meal." He smirked after offering the solution.

The thought of taking Eddie made me chuckle. "Coop be serious for a second. Eddie? Really?"

Eddie and Coop had become friends in college. Eddie was... Eddie, and the antithesis to everything that Coop was. He was not the kind of guy you took to refined events where you had to dress up and display manners. You barely wanted to take Eddie to wing night at the sports bar.

"Why does it have to be me?" Coop looked at me like he knew I was hiding something. I guess I better come clean or he was going to keep trying to finagle his way out of this.

"So, about that. I wasn't completely honest in my message this morning."

Coop's eyes turned into slits when he narrowed his gaze at me. Before he could get me to confess, the waiter showed up with our drinks. The minute he sat mine on the table, I reached for it and took a healthy swallow.

"Explain." Coop had his hand on his glass, but he hadn't yet drunk anything.

"Okay, listen, I didn't want to ask this over voicemail, but I don't just want you to go to the wedding with me... I was hoping I could persuade you to go as my boyfriend."

I braced for his response. It didn't take long at all.

"Fuck no!" Coop raised his glass to his lips, but then pulled it away again. "We've been friends for so long, who would believe we were a couple?" Finally, he put the glass back to his lips and drank the amber colored liquor.

I wasn't sure if I should be offended that he balked at the idea of us being a couple, even if it was going to be make believe. "We've been best friends since middle school, Coop, you have to do this for me. I can't show up alone."

For a minute he sat there nursing his drink. "Why do you care if that assclown is going to be at the wedding? He wears cheap suits and he's always trying to act like he's smarter than everyone else in the room because he's a scientist."

Even though he was talking about Patrick, his comments made me laugh. "That's not true... his suits are not cheap."

There was that smirk again.

Our dinner arrived and Coop cut off a piece of his steak and put it on my plate. I always used to order something different, but then wanted what he had so he started automatically giving me a small portion without me having to ask. Once he put the steak on my plate, I reached over and scooped up the sour cream meant for his baked potato, knowing he hated the stuff. Then Coop helped himself to some of my creamed spinach. We ate and talked some more, leaving the topic of the wedding and him pretending to be my fake boyfriend off the table for now. We always had fun catching up during our weekly dinners, and I didn't want to spoil it.

At the end of the night, after he helped me into my coat, I turned and grabbed his arm before he could step away.

"Coop... please just think about it. You'd be doing me a huge favor."

He stared at me for a few seconds, his blue eyes roaming over my face. "Okay... I'll think about it." He gave me a warm smile.

"Thank you." I stepped towards him and gave him a hug. I could smell the clean scent of his aftershave when he embraced me. He kissed my cheek. When he pulled away, my cheek felt warm where his lips had just been. He'd never done that before.

# CHAPTER 3

## Cooper

After dinner with Macy, I really needed another drink.

I'd seen her walk into the restaurant before she noticed me. When she greeted the host and let him remove her jacket, I couldn't take my eyes off of her. It was like I was seeing her for the first time. My body's reaction to her had me seriously wondering what was going on in my head. Thankfully, things had started to feel normal between us, but the minute she hugged me, normal went out the window again when I kissed her on the cheek. We hugged often, but I'd never kissed Macy anywhere.

I called Eddie, knowing he'd be up for a nightcap, especially if I was paying.

He met me at our usual hangout. This dingy little dive bar we discovered a number of years ago.

"So, what's going on?" Eddie swilled his beer while talking. The sight wasn't pretty.

"You usually call me to go for a drink when you're having women problems. Not like I know anything about that." He'd nearly finished his first beer already.

I hadn't touched mine. It sat in front of me with foam running down the side of the glass mug. "It's just Macy, still has feelings for that dick of an ex-boyfriend. If they get back together, that bastard is only going to break her heart again." I fingered the glass.

"Why do you care if Macy gets hurt?" Eddie sat his empty beer mug on the bar.

"Because she's my best friend." Irritation burrowed itself into my tone.

"Nah man. I think it's more than that." He folded his arms across his chest and gave me a smug look.

I looked away from him. "What are you talking about?"

"You know what I'm talking about. Don't play dumb. It's more than that. Lately, you've become overly protective about her... be honest, you're in love with her."

I wanted to punch him for saying that. "I don't know what you're talking about." My beer now had all my attention. I picked it up and drank down some of the cold brew while trying to forget what he'd just said. I couldn't be in love with Macy.

"Yeah you do. Admit it. You're in love with Macy. It's cool. She's a cool chick. You could do worse."

My head whipped around and I glared at him. "What's that supposed to mean?"

"Whoa. Calm down. See. See..." Eddie gestured and pointed with his hands. "That's what I'm talking about. Look how you reacted?"

A charged silence filled the air.

"I was just stating a fact. You could and have done worse. I think it's great if you love her... Maybe you should tell her."

Eddie had stated things so matter of fact. Was I in love with Macy? I mean, I certainly seemed to be attracted to her. Of course, I loved her like you would a friend... what if I was starting to have romantic feelings for her? You didn't just tell your best friend of sixteen years that you were in love with them. That would change everything. Was I ready for things to change between us?

"Earth to Coop."

I looked at Eddie.

He leaned forward. "What are you going to do?"

I wasn't sure. Ever since this morning I'd known something was different, but I'd tried my hardest not to acknowledge it, and now that Eddie had ripped away the blinders I was trying to hold on to, I had no choice but to see what was staring me in the face. I cared for Macy, and it was possible I loved her.

"Well... one thing is for certain... Macy doesn't need another stuffed shirt asshole as a boyfriend. She needs someone that can show her how to loosen up, forget about the rules."

"You gonna do that for her?" There was Eddie being a smart mouth.

"Yeah, I think I could be the guy for the job." A lightbulb went off in my head when I realized I had the perfect opportunity to show Macy that there was more than friendship between us. She wanted me to pretend to be her boyfriend for the wedding. It was the perfect time for me to show her that I was what she needed.

I was already off my barstool and reaching for my wallet. "Eddie, I'm sorry. I gotta go but stay and have some more drinks on me." I took a fifty-dollar bill from my wallet and placed it on top of the bar.

On the drive to Macy's I started concocting my plan. I had the advantage, because I'd known Macy for years. I knew her, everything about her. I was going to take her to that wedding and when I was finished, she would have forgotten that Patrick ever existed.

I stopped and bought two hot chocolates before I got to her apartment, because I knew she loved to drink the stuff when it was cold outside. When she answered my incessant knocking, she was tightening the belt on her robe. "Coop?"

I glanced down at her long, shapely legs, and walked past her into the living room. Now that I'd stopped trying to block all of the fantasies of the two of us from running through my head, all I could think about was her legs wrapped around my waist as I drove into her.

"So how long until the wedding? I figured I'd come over now so we could get a jump on things." When I turned around to face her, she had a huge grin plastered on her face.

"Really?"

I nodded and she rushed over to me and threw her arms around my neck. "Thank you so much. I owe you big time."

I was unable to hug her back since I had the hot beverage containers in my hands. "Careful."

"Oh, sorry." She pulled back and I handed her one.

"So, when is the wedding?" I sat my hot chocolate on the counter and removed my jacket.

Macy walked over to the sofa with her hot chocolate and tucked her leg beneath her. I followed her over and sat.

"The wedding isn't actually for a week and a half, on Christmas Eve, but Jennifer planned a wedding week."

I rolled my eyes.

"We have to be at the lodge in a few days." Macy sipped at her hot chocolate.

When she scooted further back on the sofa, her robe fell open to reveal her silken thigh. My dick hardened.

"Why don't I get my notepad and we can make a plan and set some rules."

Only Macy would want to create some rules. That's fine. She could set all the rules she wanted. I had no plans to stick to any of them. I had my own agenda.

"Good. I was just thinking that we needed to get our story straight on when things shifted between us."

Macy left the room to grab a notepad and a pen. When she returned, she was already scribbling. "Okay, rule number one..."

I pretty much agreed to all of her silly rules. You would have thought that she was cramming for a test, the way she jotted down everything.

While she wrote them down, I stole glances at her, trying to figure out when things had changed. When had I developed feelings for her and hadn't noticed?

Suddenly, I was reminded of something that happened last month during Thanksgiving at her parents' house. Her family is practically my family considering they took care of me after my parents abandoned me.

Macy had only been broken up with Patrick for about a month and was still wallowing a bit. I have it on good authority, her parents weren't so fond of Patrick. Macy's older sister, Monica thought he was conceited. Anyways, we're all sitting there at the dinner table when her mother said, 'Wouldn't it be something if the two of you ended up together after all this time?' Referring to me and Macy.

Macy and I had laughed it off, but clearly something had been triggered that day. It's was like something had been lying dormant within my heart and was cracked open by those words. It certainly would account for the dreams and my feelings. As I looked at her, I realized I wasn't as afraid of wanting her as I had been before. Didn't most people want a relationship where their significant other was their best friend?

If I could have that with Macy...

Well, now that I convinced myself. Now I would need to convince her.

Once we finished going over everything, I stood to leave.

"Coop, thanks so much again, for agreeing to do this for me."

She wasn't getting off that easy.

"Isn't there one thing you're forgetting?"

Macy looked back down at the yellow legal pad in her hands and flipped through the few pages of her meticulous hand-written notes. "I don't think so."

"Don't we need to see if we have chemistry?" I stared at her.

"How would we measure that?" She looked up at me in confusion.

"A kiss. I think we need to practice. No one's going to believe we're a couple if we don't kiss."

"I really don't think that's necessary." Macy tried to edge away. "Remember, one of the rules is no heavy PDA."

I caught her wrist, and our gazes met and held. "At some point over the course of the week, we may have to kiss. You want this to be believable right?"

She nodded.

"Then kiss me."

Macy stood there suddenly looking like an inexperienced teenage girl.

I stepped closer and cupped her face in my hands. When she shut her eyes, I couldn't help staring at her for a few seconds. I pressed my lips against hers. Almost instantly, her soft, plump lips parted. My tongue swept inside the warm cave of her mouth. I closed my eyes and savored the taste of her. My tongue explored every nook and cranny. The taste of chocolate was on her tongue. The moment I deepened the kiss, she pulled away.

Macy wouldn't meet my eyes. She panted for a moment, trying to regain her breath.

"Good practice." I licked my lower lip.

She simply nodded.

"I should be going." I grabbed my coat off the dining room chair. "You should get some sleep. I'll see you in a few days."

It was clear she was still trying to process the kiss. I pulled her into my body and kissed her forehead. "Bye."

I walked out the door without looking back. She didn't have to say anything. I knew she was affected by our kiss. On the walk to my car, I knew one thing for certain. After that kiss, I knew I wanted Macy even more.

# CHAPTER 4

## Macy

It's been three days since Coop insisted we practice kissing and I haven't been able to get the kiss out of my head. I'd imagined kissing him before... I just wasn't expecting it to be so damn good. As I waited for him to pull up so we could head to the lodge, I rubbed my bottom lip.

*Okay, no more thinking about it.*

I dropped my hand to my side.

When I looked out the window, I saw Coop's black Mercedes G-Wagon pull up. I took a deep breath and grabbed my bag. By the time I got downstairs, he was headed towards the entrance of my apartment complex.

"I was just about to come up and get you."

Coop looked relaxed in some jeans and a navy colored crewneck sweater. My eyes raked his body briefly, and I chastised myself for ogling my friend. *Stop.*

What was wrong with me?

He came over and kissed me on the cheek, while taking my bag. I quickly stepped away and walked to the car. "Hey." I threw over my shoulder, avoiding eye contact.

The trunk opened and he put my bag inside. I opened the door and got in the passenger side. When he got in on the driver's side, I gave him a small smile, trying not to make things weird.

"Buckle up." He instructed me.

I hastily put on my seatbelt while he pulled away from the curb and into traffic.

"Let's go over the rules once more." That would help me calm my nerves and stop being a bundle of nervous energy. After all it was just Coop. We'd been friends for too long. Things didn't need to be weird.

"Rule number one?"

Coop kept his gaze trained on the road. He didn't immediately respond.

"Coop?"

"Do we really need these rules?" He looked over at me when he came to a stop light.

"They'll make it easier to get through the week. Plus, Patrick needs to think he still has a shot. If things look too serious..." I wasn't going to get into all that. "Rule number one?"

Coop huffed and grudgingly told me rule number one. "No heavy PDA."

I smiled. "Rule number 2?"

"If Patrick comes around while it's just the two of us... make an excuse to leave." Coop's knuckles tightened on the steering wheel and his voice had a slight edge when he said that rule.

I decided I wasn't going to read anything into it. Coop had told me plenty of times that he didn't like Patrick.

"Rule number three?"

"No pet names. Snookums." Coop chuckled and sported a huge grin when he said the horrible pet name, in his attempt to be funny.

"That's exactly why that is a rule." I couldn't help giggling just a little. "I hope you haven't used that on any of your girlfriends or that you won't in the future."

"That God-awful name?" He guffawed. "No, I would never use that... If I give a woman a pet name, it won't be anything fluffy and cute. It will let her know exactly what I think about her."

I was dying to know just what he would call his woman. My face felt flushed and I had to squeeze my knees together when suddenly thoughts of what Coop might call a woman in the throes of passion filled my head.

Quickly, I reached up and turned on the radio. *Enough of that.* I swallowed. Flipping through the stations, I finally settled on some old school R & B.

After that last rule, I was afraid to go over the rest.

"No more rules review?" He said it in a slightly mocking tone. Coop cut his eye at me.

"No. I think you got it." I didn't look over at him. I kept my gaze trained on the road. We'd just got onto the highway.

While we listened to the satellite radio, we talked off and on about work. I was grateful we had a topic of conversation that shouldn't conjure up any dirty or inappropriate thoughts.

After changing to another station, Westlife's 'Swear It Again' began to play. I totally lost it. I hadn't heard this song in forever. "Oh, my goodness. Do you remember this song?"

When we were in high school, I had a huge obsession with British boy bands from the 90s and early 2000s, because of my older sister who used to listen to them when I was younger: Take That, Boyzone, Five, BBMak. Westlife had been far my favorite.

I turned the volume up and began to sing along. I interrupted my singing to ask Coop once again about this song. "Don't you remember this song?"

"Nope."

I wasn't sure if he was lying or telling the truth, but I didn't care. I resumed singing.

***

About an hour later, we pulled through the gates of the Oak Brook Mills Lodge. Snow had been cleared from the road. Open fields, covered in snow, lay on either side of the road that led to the main entrance of the lodge. The landscape was picturesque and looked like it belonged on a postcard or in a Hallmark movie.

I was barely out of the car, when I heard someone squeal and shout my name. "Macy."

Jennifer was rushing towards me when I looked up. You'd have thought we hadn't just seen each other a little over a week ago. Since she was the bride and this was her week, I let her be a little extra.

"Hey, girl."

We hugged each other. Jennifer pulled away and smiled at me.

"I'm so glad you're here. This week is going to be so much fun."

When Coop came around the car, Jennifer's smile fell away and she rolled her eyes. "Hey Coop."

"Jennifer."

I snickered while he grabbed the bags. Coop and I met Jennifer in college. She'd had a thing for Coop, but when he turned her down cold, she hadn't liked that. Ever since then there had been no love lost between them.

Kai, her soon-to-be husband walked up. "Hey, thought I'd find you out here." He pulled her into his side and kissed the side of her head.

The minute Jennifer had introduced me to Kai, I knew wedding bells would one day be in the future. The man doted on her and worshipped the ground she walked on. Things that were must haves for her. If a man wasn't fawning all over her, Jennifer thought there was something wrong with him. I love that she had a healthy dose of self-confidence, but sometimes I think she took it a bit far.

"You guys look happy." I smiled at the couple.

They say that couples start to look alike after they've been together for some time, but Jennifer and Kai already resembled each other. Their beautiful Black skin was a warm tawny beige. Both had light freckles that ran across the bridge of their nose. Their hair was a dark brown. Kai was nearly as tall as Coop. Jennifer was curvy and stood at about five foot four. It was their matching smiles that really clenched it. The two of them glowed they radiated so much happiness.

"Hey Coop. I didn't know you were coming." Kai greeted Coop with a fist bump.

"Last minute, change of plans." He answered the question without looking at me.

We headed inside. The first thing I saw when we entered was the huge spruce that dominated the lobby. I inhaled the fresh pine scent. Red and white ornaments decorated the tree.

"Are most of the other bridal party here?" I tried to ask the question without sounding thirsty. The minute I went to look around the lobby, my eyes landed on Patrick and a woman that must have been his plus one.

We saw each other at the same time. He grabbed her hand and they walked towards our group. Patrick was tall with broad shoulders. His russet brown skin shined under the overhead lights. His hair was cut into a fade, and he was clean shaven. He wore a suit. At that moment, Coop's comment about Patrick wearing cheap suits flitted into my head and I had to suppress a giggle.

His date made me swallow any laughter that had been bubbling to the surface. The Latina beauty had gorgeous black hair that fell to her waist. She was the same height as Jennifer. The dress she wore, made me wonder if she knew that it was winter. The deep v-neck of the halter dress went clear to her navel, and it was skintight. Was she walking the red carpet at an award's show later?

I was being a hater. I didn't like the way jealousy looked on me. In my skinny jeans, Uggs and wool sweater, I felt invisible. Most of the men in the lobby were craning their necks to get a good look at her.

"Hi Macy." Patrick reached out and shook my hand.

Briefly, I looked at him, but my gaze skittered back to his date.

"This is Celeste, my girlfriend."

*Girlfriend?*

My voice sounded hollow in my own ears when I addressed her and shook the perfectly manicured hand, she extended to me. "Hi."

Did she know I was his ex?

For a minute, an awkward silence descended on all of us, before I remembered that I wasn't here alone. Coop, my secret weapon was standing next to me.

"You remember Coop. We're dating. He's my boyfriend."

Thankfully, I didn't have too long to think about what an idiot I sounded like because Jennifer's shriek pierced the air. "Since when?" The wild-eyed, incredulous look she leveled at me and then Coop was comical.

"Yeah, babe. Since when?" Coop put his arm around my waist and tugged me into his side. I looked over at him and saw the amusement that was barely concealed beneath his grin. I wanted to throat punch him for playing games.

"We'll share that story later. Right now, we should probably check in." Without another word, I grabbed Coop's hand and dragged him towards the check-in counter.

# CHAPTER 5

## Cooper

The moment we reached the room, I descended into laughter. Poor Macy. I thought I was going to have to pick her jaw up off the floor when she spotted Patrick's new girlfriend. The woman was a looker, I'll give her that, but she had nothing on my Macy.

She punched me in the arm. "That wasn't funny, Coop." I sounded like a brainless, idiot back there."

"You did fine." I carried our bags into the bedroom with Macy on my heels.

"Did you see her? How am I supposed to compete with that?" She was staring at herself in the full-length mirror.

Why was she trying to compete at all? She didn't need to.

I dropped our luggage onto the ground and came up behind her.

"Stop doing that?"

Macy's gaze locked on mine in the mirror.

"Look at yourself." I nodded at her reflection. "You want to know what I see when I look at you?"

She nodded but didn't say anything.

"I see a sexy, vivacious woman, who is in a league of her own. Any man that looks at you wishes you were theirs."

I cut myself off before I could say more. I wanted to tell her how for the past three days I've thought about her smile, those impossibly long legs being wrapped around me when I pinned her to a wall and fucked her, even her analytical mind that sometimes drove me crazy, I found sexy.

"Coop..."

"It's true. Now stopping being worried about whatever her name is." I stepped away from the mirror and dropped down onto the bed. I ran my hand through my hair.

"Only Jennifer would plan a wedding week."

I turned to look at the pillows to grab one of the chocolate mints, and saw some kind of paper laying on underneath. I leaned across the bed and pulled it towards me.

Macy laughed and came and sat next to me on the bed. "Jennifer's our friend. Try to be nice this week."

"No, Jennifer is your friend. I only tolerate her for your sake." I corrected Macy while unwrapping the chocolate and perusing the paper.

"She's not that bad."

I snorted. "We'll agree to disagree, but I'll be civil since her big day is coming up." I ate the chocolate.

"Looks like she has the week planned out. Dinner tonight in the restaurant..." I looked at my watch. "In about an hour and a half. Tomorrow, the Bachelor party consists of Cognac tasting and Cuban cigars. Nice. The bachelorette party is going to be a cooking class. That night there will be the Dirty Santa gift exchange, which she told us about in advance so we could bring our gifts."

"You remembered to pack yours, right?"

"Yes mom." I said jokingly.

Macy punched me in the arm.

My gaze traveled down the page. "They're doing a talent night, the night before the wedding." I snorted. "I doubt either of us will be participating in that."

Macy took the itinerary out of my hand. "Let me see that." Her eyes roamed over the schedule.

"Why don't you participate in talent night. Your voice is pretty decent."

I didn't respond.

Macy tossed the itinerary to the side and lay back on the bed and looked up at the ceiling. I lay back on the bed beside her. "I actually feel bad for Kai, poor guy has to be saddled with her the rest of his life."

Macy cracked up and elbowed me in the side. "Stop."

When our laughter subsided, we both lay there. Macy broke the silence. "We should probably start getting ready for dinner."

"Yeah."

*Fuck dinner.* I wish we could just stay in the hotel room the whole night, order room service, and watch TV. I reminded myself that at dinner I would get to be Macy's boyfriend. That got me moving.

"I'll let you get the bathroom first." I left the bedroom and went to the living room and clicked on the TV. If I stayed in there where I could hear the shower running, I would torture myself. Even now, sitting out here. I kept imagining I was the soap or the sponge moving all over Macy's body. By the time she finished her shower and left the bathroom, my dick was hard from all the fantasizing.

"It's all yours."

When I walked into the room, Macy was wearing only a towel. We'd seen each other in various states of undress over the years. Obviously, now that my feelings had changed it was very hard to see her wearing next to nothing, and not want to touch her, taste her.

*Grab your things and go into the bathroom.*

I pulled my toiletries from my bag and headed into the bathroom.

***

On the way to dinner, in one of the on-site restaurants that had a private room for our party, Macy took my hand.

"For show. In case anyone sees us." She whispered.

I nodded and squeezed her hand.

Macy took my breath away. She wore this short, sexy, white cashmere sweater dress. It had a plunging back. Next to her skin, the color of the dress really popped. With the stiletto heels she was wearing in the same color, her legs appeared even longer. The sight made my mouth water.

"Remember the rules." Macy gave me a look.

Before I could respond, Jennifer and Kai joined as we headed inside the restaurant. The hostess led us to the private room reserved for our party.

"Hi." Jennifer looked at our hands.

"Can't wait to hear this story." She said to no one in particular as we filed into the room. The rest of the bridal party was already seated.

*Great.* We were seated directly across from Patrick and his date.

I pulled Macy's chair out for her.

Once the waiter came and took our orders, everyone settled in and conversations began around the table. Macy relaxed a little bit and leaned into me. I put my arm across the back of her chair. I could smell the coconut shampoo she'd used in the shower, and whatever fruity scent had been in her bodywash, and suddenly I was thinking about licking her. I cleared my throat and tried to stay focused on the conversation I was involved in.

The wine arrived and Macy reached for hers. I leaned over and whispered in her ear. "You doing okay?"

She nodded and sipped from her glass. "Yeah."

I kissed the side of her head.

A short while later, dinner arrived. The minute our dishes were set on the table, Macy and I began our routine. She took the sour cream off my plate that came with the baked potato. I scooped some of the rice pilaf from hers. I didn't realize we had an audience until Celeste spoke.

"That's so sweet." Celeste cooed when I finished placing a piece of my steak on Macy's plate.

"Since college they've done that, it's sickening." Jennifer made a gagging noise.

"I think it's sweet too, Jennifer." One of the other bridesmaids said with a smile.

Jennifer brushed her comment aside. "Well I'm dying to hear how the two of you ended up hooking up. You've been friends since you were kids. Why now? How did it happen?" Jennifer's suspicious gaze volleyed between the two of us.

"Yeah, I have to admit, I'm curious myself." Patrick wore a bemused expression.

*I'll just bet he was. What an asshat.* I mean, what did Macy see in him?

"I'll tell the story." I volunteered. Out of the corner of my eye, Macy tensed. I rubbed her leg beneath the table.

"Where to start..." I rubbed my hands together and grinned. "Most of you know we go way back, as Jennifer mentioned. Well, it was right after Thanksgiving, and Mace, she stayed back at her parents' place in Naperville, an extra day. Later that night, while she was returning to Chicago, her battery died..." In my periphery, I could see Macy having an internal hissy fit, because I wasn't telling the story she'd concocted for the two of us.

Yes, I was deviating from the plan. She'd told me to keep the story simple when we talked about it the other night, but I just couldn't help myself.

"She calls me up and asks me to come wait with her, so she can sit in my car until the tow truck arrives. We'd just gotten a good amount of snow at that time and the temperatures were below thirty degrees. I race out there, because I don't want her sitting alone, in the middle of nowhere, in a cold car." When I looked out at my audience, all the women were hanging on my every word.

"The minute I arrive, Mace gets in my car. She's freezing. Her teeth are chattering. I crank up the heat to help her get warm. She'd forgotten her gloves, so I take her hands in mine, which were ice cold. I'm massaging her fingers... we start talking and laughing about some old memory and..." I turned my attention back to Macy and look her in the eye.

"I looked at her, and I just knew we should be together... when I stared into her eyes, I could see she knew it too. And here we are."

The story barely had a minute to breathe and then Jennifer opened her big mouth.

"Girl, why didn't you call me if you were stuck on the side of the road?" Jennifer questioned.

When I tore my gaze away from Macy's and looked around the table, one of Jennifer's bridesmaids was wiping her eyes.

"That was beautiful."

"Yeah, if it wasn't true, I almost wouldn't believe it myself." Macy gave me a false smile. Without thinking about it. I leaned over and kissed her on the mouth. I lingered just long enough for it not to be a chaste kiss.

There was a collective sigh from some of the women at the table.

When I pulled back, her eyes glittered dangerously, but there was also something else there. I didn't care about pissing her off. I'd always planned to toss her carefully crafted rules right out the window.

Everyone else was eating up our friendship turned romance with a spoon and asking for seconds. Everyone, but Jennifer and Patrick. That was fine, because I gave two fucks about Patrick, and Jennifer was just jealous all the attention wasn't focused on her.

Quickly, Jennifer changed the topic. "Remember to sign up for talent night you guys. More guests will be here since it's the night before the wedding so it should be fun.

# CHAPTER 6

## Macy

"What was that at dinner? You broke rules one and four." I took off my earring while I stared at the back of Coop's head.

"What was rule number four again?" He was seated on the bed, watching a sports recap.

"You know what rule number four is. Don't embellish. That whopper of a lie you told at dinner on how we got together was... was..."

"Brilliant." He turned and looked at me. "One of Jennifer's friends was bought to tears. Do I need to remind you this whole thing is a lie?"

I just stared at him without saying anything.

"This is supposed to look and sound real right?"

"Yes." I answered him grudgingly, I hated when he was right.

"Boom. I just made us look legit. Mic drop." He made the gesture like he was dropping a microphone on the ground and got up from the bed. "You're welcome."

Coop walked into the bathroom and didn't close the door. The next thing I knew I could hear him taking a piss.

"Close the door."

"I'm not taking a shit, Mace. You've never cared if I've closed the door before." Once he finished, I heard him zip up his pants and flush, followed by running water.

When he stepped back into the bedroom I looked away.

Even though he was being infuriating. I had to admit he was right. I'd noticed Patrick's face during Coop's story, and he looked jealous. Score one for me.

"Tomorrow, can you try and stick to the rules, please?"

"I'll think about it." He still sported a self-satisfied smile.

"Coop." I whined.

"Scout's honor, I will stick to the rules that you laid out." He said the words and even had an earnest look on his face, but I knew he was holding one of his hands behind his back.

"You have your fingers crossed behind your back." I was trying hard not to laugh at his antics.

"No, I don't." A grin broke out across his face, and I got a glimpse of the boy I met all those years ago.

"Okay, I will try..." He put the emphasis on the word try, "to stick to your rules tomorrow, but I can't make any promises."

I shrugged. "So, I just have to be okay with that?"

"Yep."

After gathering my pajamas and toiletries I went into the bathroom, doubtful that Coop would stick to any of the rules.

When I came out, he was seated at the edge of the bed again, watching a replay of some football game.

"All yours." I was wearing some silk pajama bottoms and a camisole, and my head scarf.

"Okay." He was still glued to the TV. It was another five minutes before he got up. He noticed me looking at the bed with a concerned look on my face. "What's wrong?" He looked at the bed.

"It's only one bed. What are we going to do?"

"We've slept in beds together before."

"A few times in college and we were both passed out drunk. This is different."

"If you say so." Coop grabbed his things and went into the bathroom.

While he was getting ready for bed, I figured out a way to divide up the bed and keep us from touching.

A practically naked Coop emerged, wearing only a pair of black boxer briefs. "That's all you're wearing to bed?"

"I didn't know I needed to dress for bed. Why are you being such a prude?"

Coop looked at the bed. "What's this?"

I'd made a divider down the middle of the bed using the extra pillows I'd found in the closet.

"This is the barrier I created to make sure we stay on our own sides of the bed." I was rather pleased with my quick thinking.

He put his hands on his hips and continued to stare at my creation. "Uh huh."

"It's going to work. This way, we don't have to worry about touching or disturbing each other when we sleep."

He simply nodded. "Which side do you want?"

"The one closest to the window."

We both walked to our sides of the bed and climbed in. Once he was beneath the covers, he turned off the TV. The light switch was on my side of the bed. When I turned it off, the room became shrouded in shadows. We lay together in the dark. The sheets rustled as Coop got comfortable.

"Your ex looked like he'd eaten a rotten egg or something after I kissed you." The triumph in his voice made me smile. Although, it felt like there was something more behind the victory that was evident in Coop's voice.

"Yeah." He had looked jealous, I agreed. "The plan is working it seems... even though you didn't stick to the rules..."

Coop only snorted in response

My curiosity got the better of me. I had to know why Coop so strongly disliked my ex. "Is there a reason you don't like Patrick?"

Without hesitating or thinking about it, Coop answered me. "The guy's a prick."

I was laying on my back, but when he said that I turned onto my side so I could move part of the pillow barrier and see him. Coop was laying on his back staring up at the ceiling with his arms behind his head. He turned his head to look at me.

Unapologetic, Coop continued. "He's smug and arrogant. You couldn't see that tonight? It's not like he tries to hide it."

I didn't say anything.

Coop smirked. "I want him to keep that sour look on his face while he thinks of me in here giving it to you good every night, wearing your ass out?" He snickered and leered at me.

I busted up laughing.

"You're so certain I'd enjoy myself."

"I know you would. I'd make you forget your own damn name." For a minute, we stared into each other's eyes. The way he'd said the words like he'd bet a million dollars on it and win, made me swallow. I looked away quickly before I could see the lust in his eyes that I was feeling deep in my womb.

Coop kept the moment from being weird by sliding into humor. He attempted to imitate my voice, while he moaned and groaned, and said things he thought I would say during sex. "Oh Coop, yeah. Just like that. Oh yeah. Coop, don't stop. Tell me my name, Coop. What's my name? Ugh." He started laughing hysterically.

I picked up one of the pillows and hit him over the head with it. He brought his arms up to protect himself. I hit him a few more times.

"You're not funny." My laughter said otherwise.

He yanked the pillow out of my grasp. Instead of putting it back in between us, he held on to it.

I lay back down. "I don't want to see your dick." My giggles were subsiding.

"I never offered, but since you said that, it makes me think you do want to see it... I know you're curious. You only have to ask." His voice was husky and teasing.

I was glad the lights were off. The moon was filtering in through the blinds, but it wasn't enough for him to see I was blushing. Besides the vivid picture his words created, the tone of his voice had me wet. I squeezed my thighs together. I'd seen Coop in gym shorts. I had an inkling of what he was packing down there. Of course, I wanted to see it. That made me press my legs together even tighter. *Stop lusting after your friend.*

I turned on my side away from him. "Good night, Coop. This conversation has turned juvenile." I smiled into my pillow.

When I shut my eyes, I lay there with the vision of Coop's dick behind my eyelids.

"Tell me something." His tone had turned serious.

My eyes popped open. "What?"

"What happens if you get everything you want? This week ends with Patrick realizing he made a mistake and he wants you to take him back?"

For a moment, I just lay there, staring at the clock on the nightstand. After nearly a minute, I turned back onto my other side to face him. Coop was now laying on his side facing me, with one of his hands beneath his pillow.

"Why do you ask?"

"Curiosity."

My gaze drifted away from his as I thought about his question.

"I mean, do you plan to take him back. Is that you want? Or do you just want to make him jealous? Want to make him regret his decision?"

Coop was asking a lot of questions. A lot of questions I didn't necessarily have answers to. When I knew Patrick was going to be at the wedding, I just knew I couldn't be here alone. Usually, I always planned things out, strategized, and looked at all possible outcomes. My love life was another matter entirely. I had not thought long and hard about what I wanted.

"I don't know... I honestly don't know."

Silence settled around us, the whir of the heater filled the room.

"Do you love him?"

My annoyance at my own indecisiveness and uncertainty made me lash out at Coop.

"Why are you asking me this?" My tone was icy. Angrily, I gripped the edge of my pillow.

He didn't seem fazed by my change in temperament. "I just want to know what you're doing this for Mace. This farce... if it's to get back a guy you're in love with... then... I can respect that."

I could tell there was more he wanted to say, but he held back.

The quiet enveloped us once more, but this time it wasn't calm or peaceful, it was fraught with my own ambivalence and indecision. I was no longer looking at him, but I could feel Coop's penetrating gaze lingering on my face.

"Good night, Mace." The bed dipped and the sheets rustled once more when he turned away.

"Good night."

Minutes later, Coop was off in dreamland, and I was pondering his questions. At the far edge of my mind, I realized there was a reason that I didn't know what I would do about Patrick, or how I would handle things if he suddenly wanted to be with me again. I squeezed my eyes shut tight and wished myself to sleep; and tried to push away the fact that the reason I didn't know was lying in bed bedside me.

# CHAPTER 7

## Cooper

When I woke up the next morning, I was spooning Macy from behind. The pillow barrier must have been demolished sometime during the night. I could tell by her even breathing that she was still asleep. My dick was nestled between her ass cheeks, seeking refuge, and I had to resist the urge to rub myself against her. I wanted to snuggle her closer. It was more than that, I wanted to wake her up and bury myself inside her. Lay between her silken thighs and spend the morning, erasing Patrick from her memory.

Thankfully, I pulled away before thoughts of molesting my friend could take shape. The ache in my balls drove me to the bathroom. In the shower, I rubbed one out. There was no way I could walk around all day with a horrible case of blue balls. I would attack someone.

When I came out of the bathroom, Macy looked over at me from the bed, and gave me an apologetic smile. "Morning."

"Morning."

I knew she wanted to apologize for being snappy with me last night, but it wasn't necessary.

"Water under the bridge." I reassured her that we were good. After sitting on the edge of the bed, I grabbed my shoes and started putting them on.

"If you hurry up and shower, we can try and grab breakfast together before the separate bachelor and bachelorette parties. Give Patrick something else to be jealous about." I gave her a lopsided smile over my shoulder.

"Good idea." She threw the covers back and got out of the bed.

When I finished putting on my shoes, I turned to look at her. She was bent over her bag with her ass in the air. My dick remembered how it felt to be cushioned against her ass, and I instantly went hard again.

"Ugh." I lay back on the bed.

"What's wrong?" Macy was still rummaging through her bag while she asked the question.

"Nothing." I sat up and stood.

"I'm going to check some emails while you're getting dressed."

In the safety of the living room, I pulled out my laptop, and responded to emails. It helped clear my head of any thoughts of Macy's ass. While I typed, I found myself thinking about the next step in my plan. I needed a grand gesture. What could grab Macy's attention? I sent my last email and closed my laptop.

I clicked the TV on while I waited for Macy to finish getting ready, hoping that one of the programs would offer up a solution to my problem.

****

Macy and I were having breakfast alone, which is the way I would have preferred it until Jennifer and Kai showed up. Christmas music quietly played in the background, and I tried to remember it was the season for giving, and maybe I should give Jennifer a break.

"Hey lovebirds." She said it mockingly and took a seat in the empty chair Kai pulled out for her.

"Jennifer." There went my appetite.

We usually only had to deal with each other in small doses, so having to put up with her for a whole week was a challenge.

"Are you ready for our cooking class?" Jennifer leaned over to Macy.

Macy finished chewing part of my French toast I'd split with her before she responded. "Yeah. I think it will be a lot of fun."

I finished off my coffee and chatted Kai up until it was time for the men and women to separate.

When it was time to leave, I wrapped my arm around Macy's waist and pulled her into my body. "Later beautiful."

I gave her a similar kiss to the one I gave her last night, in front of Jennifer and Kai. When I pulled away, Macy wore a shy look. She wouldn't look me in the eye, but I saw her lick her bottom lip. The gesture made me feel possessive. I kissed her forehead. "See you in the evening." I whispered the words into her skin and stepped away. I wanted her thinking of me all day, while we were apart. I wanted to be under her skin the way she was under mine.

***

Thankfully, I didn't have to lay eyes on Patrick until I entered the room where the cognac tasting would happen. Comfy, leather armchairs were arranged around a table. He was already seated in one of the chairs, talking to another one of Kai's groomsmen. I purposely took the chair next to his.

Once we were all seated a lean older man stepped into the center of the circle and stood near the table.

I was glad there wouldn't be time for small talk.

"My name is Lawrence. I will be your host. I hope you are all prepared to enjoy a fun, relaxing afternoon." Immediately, after his introduction, he launched into the presentation.

"We import liquors from all over the world for our tastings. You gentlemen are here for our Cognac tasting and Cuban cigars."

Kai had good taste for choosing this activity for his bachelor outing.

"Cognac is produced in Cognac, a little town in the Charente department of France. The whole region of Nouvelle-Aquitaine produces the liquor. Each tulip glass contains a sample of the different cognacs we'll be sampling today."

The expert began pointing to the various glasses lining the table. "Today, we will be sampling Courvoisier, Rémy Martin, Otard, Camus, Hennessy, Martell, Delamain and Meukov." He pointed to the last glass.

A few waiters materialized out of nowhere carrying glasses on trays and began to pass out the first sampling.

The resident expert picked up one of the glasses. While he waited on everyone to be served. He continued with his lesson. "Cognac is made by distilling wine and then aging it for at least two years in oak barrels, but not just any oak. It must be French oak, which comes from the Tronçais or Limousin forests."

Everyone had their glass. "Gentlemen, let's sample our first tasting, the Otard."

I tipped my glass back and drank some of the liquor, savoring it on my tongue.

"You should notice citrus, candied fruit, spices, maybe even a hint of leather in the velvety texture." Many finished the first sampling in record time, and we moved onto the next one.

The tasting was enjoyable. I nearly forgot I'd been seated next to Patrick over the last few hours.

Once, we'd tasted all of them, we were each served a glass of our choosing to enjoy with the Cohibe Behike BHK 52 Cuban cigars. I closed my eyes and inhaled the fragrant smoke, and then Patrick's voice shattered my bliss.

"So, Coop, how's business going?" Patrick puffed on his cigar and waited for my response.

"It's Cooper."

"But everyone's been calling you Coop."

"I know. My friends call me Coop." I blew a perfect smoke ring into the air and gave him a fuck you smile.

Patrick dropped his voice and leaned closer. "Listen, I know the history I have with Macy must be weird, now that you're dating her..."

I wanted to punch him in the face. Besides him initially breaking her heart, he was my rival for Macy's affections, even though he didn't know it. So, we would never be pals, chums, buddies, amigos, friends or anything. I gave him a death stare until he stopped talking. There was no need for me to say thing else. I rested my head against the back of the chair, and leisurely enjoyed the cognac and the cigar, while wondering how Macy was doing. Hopefully, she didn't end up in any catfights with Celeste.

Patrick went back to talking to the groomsman on the other side of him. At some point in their conversation, that I kept getting bits and pieces of since we were seated so close, he mentioned that he planned to participate in the talent night.

The minute he mentioned it, I realized I had my grand gesture, the talent competition. It was a perfect idea. Macy was already under the assumption that I wouldn't be participating so she would be shocked when she saw me on stage. *Thanks Patrick.*

# CHAPTER 8

## Macy

I was actually a pretty decent cook, but during the cooking lesson my skills were not showcased. I was looking super inept, and I had Coop to thank. Between the pet name that was equal parts sexy and sweet that he uttered to me before we parted and the forehead kiss, my mind was a muddled mess. I didn't know what was up and what was down.

We hadn't even gotten to the souffles yet, where you expected a level of error since it was a hard dish to make. I was messing up simple stuff. Why did it have to be a French cooking class?

"Girl, what's going on?" Jennifer eyed my coq au vin with a mixture of shock and puzzlement. "What is it?"

I wiped sweat from my brow with the back of my arm. "It's... it's the dish... the one that we're supposed to make." Peering around the room, I realized my dish would be the one labeled one of these things is not like the others. Everyone's dish looked edible, but mine.

Of course, Celeste's dish looked picture perfect like it could be on someone's Instagram for stunning food porn. At that moment she looked over at my station.

I could feel my cheeks burning with embarrassment and looked away.

"Hey, don't feel bad. I've recently been taking cooking classes. Up until a couple months ago, I burned everything I touched."

Why did she have to be so likeable? I wanted to hate her, but so far, she seemed really cool, like someone I'd want to hang out with, go shopping with.

"Thanks."

She smiled and went back to working on the next dish. The chef walked by my cooking station and shook his head. My shoulders slumped in defeat. I did not want to make the next dish.

While I was busy feeling sorry for myself, Jennifer came and stood beside me. "So, be honest with me… you're just trying to make Patrick jealous right? You two aren't really together?"

I pretended like I didn't hear her. "What?" I gave her a quick look, but then focused my attention back on the ingredients and bowls that sat on the counter waiting for me to whip up something incredible.

"You and Coop. It's just a joke, right?"

I wasn't sure why her guessing at the truth of our charade made me a little angry. Jennifer was my best girlfriend, but I lied straight through my teeth. "No, it's not a joke. We're together."

Hopefully, my nose wouldn't begin to grow several inches.

She leaned in closer. "Okay then spill… how big is it?" Her voice dropped to a whisper on the last part.

I looked at her stupidly. "How big is what?"

"His thing…" She used her hands to gesture. Pushing them closer together and pulling them further apart. "His dick. How big is it?"

For a second, I was flustered, and then I remembered last night, when Coop teased, and I started laughing, which obviously wasn't a good sign.

"That bad? He's got a tiny dick? Damn. He's so hot. What a waste." She shook her head.

"Oh God. No. That's not why I was laughing. Sorry. Private joke." I had to fix this. Coop would never forgive me if I let Jennifer of all people believe he was not well hung.

"It's ginormous. So big. Long, thick. And he really knows how to use it."

Jennifer's jaw looked like it had come unhinged her mouth was open so wide.

"Okay, let me get back to this so I can hopefully get one thing right." I took Jennifer by the shoulder and turned her towards her station and gave her a little push.

Without any more interruptions, I managed to follow the chef's instructions exactly. When I pulled my souffle from the oven, it was a wonderful surprise when it didn't immediately fall. I held my breath, willing it to stay perfect.

A quick glance over at Jennifer's station told me she was struggling. Her face was scrunched up in displeasure as she looked at her sunken souffle.

I couldn't help feeling a small moment of pride over finally getting something right out of the whole meal.

"Good job."

I looked up and found Celeste smiling at my creation.

"Mine fell. What's your secret? How did you get it to stay put?"

I didn't want to be a catty bitch. One of those women that was pissed because another woman had the man... I thought I wanted.

So, I looked up at her and smiled. "I honestly don't know. I guess just sheer determination and willpower. I was praying the whole time." After I made the joke, we both laughed.

After all the cooking, when we sat down to eat our meals, I ended up siting next to Celeste. I found out she was a doctor, still in her residency. We both attended the same spin class, but on different days.

Jennifer kept giving me side eye the whole time, like I was dining with the enemy, but Celeste hadn't done anything wrong to me. She was just dating Patrick after he dumped me. How I was feeling about that or even felt about him, had nothing to do with her.

When Celeste got pulled into another conversation, I picked up my wine glass and sipped. After getting to know her a little, I found myself thinking about the questions that Coop had asked me that night. What did I want? What was my end game with Patrick? Right now, I was starting to look like the woman I hated, with all my scheming and plotting to win him back when he was with someone else now. I slumped down in my seat and looked at Celeste out of the corner of my eye. He was her man now. If Patrick did have a change of heart and suddenly wanted to be with me again, what was I going to do? Take him?

Days ago, there was a clear-cut answer to that question, but now Coop kept popping up every time I thought about a future with any man, making things even more complicated.

# CHAPTER 9

## Cooper

We rejoined the women in one of the meeting rooms that was decorated in tasteful holiday décor. Red ribbons and garland were wound around the pillars and columns. A Christmas tree covered in white twinkling lights and sparsely decorated with red ornaments stood in a corner. Gifts were under the tree.

"Hey beautiful." I made sure that clown heard me when I greeted Macy. Patrick looked over his shoulder at us as he passed.

Macy's gaze briefly followed him to where Celeste waited for him. Jealousy gnawed at my gut. When she stared back at me, I pretended like everything was okay.

"How was the cooking class?"

"Awful." She shook her head and didn't offer up any more of an explanation.

Jennifer walked by and looked down at my crotch. Was my fly open? I looked down. *Nope. All zipped up.*

It felt like she was undressing me with her eyes. Eventually, she turned away and walked over to Kai.

"What was that about?" My eyebrows were raised in question.

"I don't know." There was something in her voice that told me she knew exactly what that was about. Quickly, she changed the subject.

"I figured you wouldn't have time, so when I went back upstairs to change after the cooking class, I grabbed your gift from your bag."

"Thank you." I put my arm around her waist.

Jennifer called everyone to attention. "Okay, let's get ready for the Dirty Santa gift exchange. All the gifts are now under the tree. Kai is going to come around with folded up numbers in a cup. Take one."

When Kai came around, Macy took a number and then I took a number. We opened the folded-up pieces of paper. I had number three. I would be one of the first people to pull a gift.

"What number did you get?" I peered over Macy's shoulder to look at her number. Her number was twelve. She would be one of the last people to pick a gift.

"Who has number one?" Jennifer looked around the room.

One of her bridesmaids stepped forward. For a few seconds, she looked at the gifts trying to figure out which one she was going to take. She plucked a small box from the pile that was wrapped in silver paper.

Everyone watched while she unwrapped it, wondering what she was about to reveal. She pulled a pair of handcuffs from the box.

There were whistles and catcalls as she rejoined her boyfriend.

"Person number two?" Jennifer called out sporting a huge grin.

Celeste approached the Christmas tree. She was smiling while she looked the gifts over. "Get something good, babe." Patrick called out.

Next to me, I waited for Macy to somehow respond to ass clown's outburst. Instead she put her arm around my waist. I snuggled her closer. Even if she'd only done it in response to Patrick, I'd take it... for now.

Celeste picked up a gift-wrapped box that was slightly larger than the one the bridesmaid had picked up. She tore off the paper and opened the lid. The blush went all the way to her hairline, before she pulled out some male enhancement pills.

Snickers rippled through the crowd. I was tempted to make a joke at Patrick's expense, but I didn't want to do anything that would affect Macy's mood right now.

Once Celeste had gone back to her spot by Patrick, I let go of Macy and walked towards the tree before Jennifer could ask who had number three.

I knew she was upset I beat her to it. A smirk curled the corner of my mouth.

"Number three." She said the words with so much attitude.

I didn't need to deliberate. I picked up a bag and tore the tape away from the opening of the bag. The minute I put my hand inside, I knew it was a book. It was wrapped in tissue paper. I pulled it from the bag and removed the paper. A hardback copy of the Kama Sutra boasting color photographs and step-by-step instructions that displayed how to perform the most difficult positions. I was pleasantly surprised. I'd never owned a copy.

When I got back by Macy's side, she looked a little mortified. I was tempted to really embarrass her and make a joke about us using it tonight. Instead, I tucked the book back into the bag and pulled her close again.

We watched as number after number stepped up to either take a gift from under the tree or steal a gift from someone else. Surprisingly, someone swiped Celeste's pills and then she came for my book. I was sad to see if go. But then I got robbed again when someone took the blindfold, feather and box of condoms I'd picked up the second time around. That was my opportunity to steal the Kama Sutra back. It was now safe with me, since it couldn't be stolen again. In my head, I kept thinking of some of the positions that were contained inside of the book and wondering what it would be like to try them out with Macy.

Maybe now wasn't the best time to think about that. I pushed the dirty thoughts away.

"Number twelve?"

Macy nervously stepped forward. She walked towards the tree cautiously, like it had a loaded gun. I wondered what she would pull from beneath the tree. There were only three gifts left.

She grabbed the last gift that had been wrapped in a bag. After she used the handles to pull apart the top, and pop the tape, she peered inside. She shut it quickly.

"You have to show us and take it out of the bag... in case the people after you want to steal it." I could tell from Jennifer's overeager energy that this was the gift that she had bought.

Macy looked at her with pleading eyes.

"You have to open it." Jennifer gave two fucks about Macy's discomfort.

After a few more seconds of hesitation, she reached into the gift bag and pulled out a large, black dildo. The mortification on her face was evident.

"The gift that keeps on giving." The groomsman that was sitting next to Patrick during the Cognac tasting, joked, before he erupted in laughter.

Jennifer had her hand over her mouth, cackling like an idiot.

More laughter rang out in the room, and people cracked jokes. Macy shoved it back in the bag and instead of coming back over to stand next to me, she walked out of the room. Quickly, I grabbed my things and went after her.

"Mace, wait."

She was only about ten feet away. Her steps slowed, and finally she stopped. I jogged over to her.

"Hey." I came to stand in front her. "You okay?"

She nodded. "I just... I don't know why I was so embarrassed. It wasn't like I was the only one that got a raunchy gift. It's just..."

"It's a dildo. I get it." We shared a laugh.

"If you'd stayed in the room maybe someone would have stolen it from you or traded you."

She didn't look that hopeful.

"Well, our gifts do somewhat compliment each other. Maybe there is something in the Kama Sutra that calls for a sex toy."

Macy shook her head at my joke and started laughing.

I was glad I made her laugh.

"Come here, beautiful." I pulled her into my body and hugged her. This time she didn't resist or go all stiff on me.

"You know there's no one around to hear you, right? It's just us."

I shrugged. "I know." I hugged her a little tighter.

"Do you want to go back inside… or do you want to just go back upstairs, order room service and binge watch some bad TV?"

"Room service and bad TV." She smiled up at me.

I put my arm around her waist, and we headed towards the elevator. "You know, once we get back to the room, we could make some time to look at this book together?"

I already knew what the answer was going to be.

"I am not looking at a sex book with you, Coop." She snickered when we got on the elevator.

"A guy can try."

We spent the rest of the evening, lazing in bed, watching TV and eating junk food. It was comforting and nice and I was glad I was getting to just spend time with her. We had a few more days here. Anything could happen.

# CHAPTER 10

## Macy

I was grateful to Coop for last night. Ever since the kiss in my apartment, things had felt strange between us. Last night, eating room service and watching movies together while laughing and talking... it was the first night where things had felt completely normal between us. We were just Mace and Coop, best friends. No weird feelings getting in the way. Maybe it was just me. I was the one being weird.

During the gift exchange last night, I knew we were supposed to be laughing and having a good time, but I felt like the butt of a joke. I certainly wasn't a prude but talking about certain things sexually in public did make me blush, so having to pull out a huge dildo embarrassed me.

Hopefully, it had all been forgotten about now, and I wouldn't be subjected to more wisecracks. Today was the rehearsal of the ceremony with the wedding coordinator and the rehearsal dinner would be held this evening. As the maid of honor, I planned to wing my speech tonight and speak from the heart. The day of the wedding I'd prepared something because I didn't want to get tongue-tied or emotional and forget what to say.

Coop was meeting me downstairs later. He wasn't in the bridal party, so he didn't need to attend the rehearsal. Once he finished some work stuff, he'd head down.

I grabbed my purse and walked into the living room. Coop was sitting at the table, deeply engrossed in whatever email or document had his attention. "I'm heading downstairs for the rehearsal."

He looked up from the screen. His blue eyes assessed me, silently asking if I was okay, I gave him a small smile.

"I'm actually feel a little stupid about last night…"

"You shouldn't. You're entitled to feel how you feel."

I appreciated him saying so.

Coop got up from his chair and came towards me.

Part of me, felt nervous. What was he about to do? When he put his arms around me and just held me, for a minute I was frozen. It took a couple seconds before I wrapped my arms around his waist and let out a breath. He smelled really good. I inhaled. I knew I shouldn't, but I couldn't help it.

Being held like this felt nice. Or did it feel nice because of who was doing the holding? Okay, my mind was doing too much mental gymnastics this morning. I was not going to unpack or examine any of that right now. I had maid of honor duties to attend to.

Coop pulled away. "I'll see you downstairs soon."

I headed downstairs, to the grand ballroom, where the reception would take place. The ceremony was being held outdoors on the terrace, but the wedding coordinator agreed we didn't need to practice outside. Thankfully, there would be about a gazillion heaters to keep us warm, while we froze, on the day of Jennifer and Kai's nuptials.

Before I could walk into the room, Patrick walked up from another direction. He was alone.

"Where's Celeste?"

I was a tiny bit flustered since neither of us had been alone since we got here.

"She decided to sleep in since she's not part of the wedding party."

"Oh."

Patrick pulled the door to the ballroom open. "Ladies first." He gestured for me to enter before him and gave me a smile.

I tried to smile, but I felt like it came out looking like a grimace or like I'd just realized I'd eaten something bad. Shouldn't I be doing my happy dance? For some reason, I wasn't elated.

We were the last of the bridal party to arrive. The coordinator lined us up, and somehow, Patrick and I got paired up to walk down the aisle together. It felt strange and wrong. I wanted to ask to be partnered with someone else, but clamped my mouth shut. Making trouble on Jennifer's big day felt wrong.

We'd gone through it once and then taken a break. I was grabbing water when Jennifer came up. "You're welcome."

I looked at her puzzled. "What should I be thanking you for?" I sipped my water.

"Because… I made sure the coordinator paired you up with Patrick, so he could see everything he's been missing up close. Like I said, you're welcome."

I spluttered into my water. "But I didn't ask you to do that. He's here with his girlfriend. I'm here with Coop."

"Funny that you referred to Celeste as Patrick's girlfriend, but you didn't refer to Coop as your boyfriend." Jennifer's lips were all twisted up.

I'd never meant to lie to her, but I also didn't want to come clean right now. Plus, I wasn't trying to fight with her during her wedding week.

"Just used to calling him Coop is all. Doesn't mean he isn't my boyfriend, which is why it was wrong for you to pair me with Patrick." I finished my water and walked away.

We'd walked through the ceremony a second time before Coop showed up and took a seat at one of the tables that had already been set up for the reception.

I tried not to look at him. I wondered what was going through his head when he saw that I was walking down the aisle with Patrick.

By the time we went through the ceremony again, I was ready to be done. Right when we finished, the coordinator came over to Patrick and I. "You make a lovely couple. Maybe soon I'll be planning your big day?"

Before either of us could respond, she smiled and walked away. Inwardly, I cringed. Had Coop heard that? When I turned, he was shoving his way out the door.

I looked up at Patrick. "I have to go."

# CHAPTER 11

## Cooper

Air, I needed it. The minute I stepped into the hallway I took a deep breath, pulling the cloyingly fragrant air into my lungs. When I came into the rehearsal and saw Macy walking down the aisle with assclown I kept reminding myself it was because they were part of the wedding party. Every minute that ticked by boiled my blood. The whole time I watched them my fists were clenched together angrily in my lap. I kept imagining the ways I would kick his ass.

I couldn't help but wonder if she'd asked to be paired with him or was it just a coincidence. At the end of the rehearsal when the wedding coordinator said they looked like the perfect couple, I was about to lose my shit, so I left. I was tired of watching Macy with Patrick, and I didn't want to be upset with her. The heart wants what the heart wants, and it was looking like it wasn't me.

I didn't like acting like a sore loser, but it wasn't like I would just be losing something inconsequential if Macy did decide that Patrick was who she wanted. I'd come to realize, the reason I was fighting so hard is that Macy had always been home for me. Ever since that day she discovered my secret, and we became friends she'd become home... and the thought of losing that, losing her, terrified me. That was a foreign feeling to me. If at the end of all of this, she decided... she decided she didn't care for me the way I cared for her, could I just go back to being friends?

I wasn't ready to consider that possibility, and I wasn't going to go off and lick my wounds yet, but I needed to regroup. I still had tonight and talent night to convince her that Patrick was all wrong for her.

Knowing that Macy was looking for me, did make me feel like an ass for avoiding her, but I needed to be by myself for a little while. It was the only thing I could do, because what I wanted to do, she wasn't ready for.

I'm sure Eddie would have had a real good laugh at my expense right about now, watching me, hiding away in hallways.

Macy needed time to figure things out. I wanted to give her that space, but I also didn't want to leave the door open for Patrick to walk back in.

I would stick to my plan.

*****

Hours later, I entered one of the smaller ballrooms where the rehearsal dinner was being held. Macy was already there and seated. She looked beautiful. She'd changed clothes. Her hair was up in some updo that showed off her elegant neck.

When I sat down beside her, I ignored everyone else.

For a second, she didn't acknowledge me. I deserved that. I took her hand in mine and kissed her knuckles. Finally, she turned and looked at me. "I'm sorry."

My gaze held hers. I wasn't going to put on a show for everyone, but Macy and I had known each other long enough that I knew she could see how sorry I was when she looked into my eyes.

She nodded and gave me a small smile before she leaned over and put her arms around my neck. I hugged her back, glad that we were okay again.

The dinner went by in a blur. There were speeches from both Jennifer and Kai's parents. Kai's brother, his best man spoke. The only speech I tuned in for was Macy's. She spoke from the heart, and it was beautiful. When she sat after giving her toast, I rubbed her back. "That was really nice."

"Thank you."

Once dinner was cleared, people started to mingle. Macy left to go talk to some of the new guests that arrived. I wandered through the crowd, casually greeting people. Occasionally, I would find her, and watch her engaged in conversation with someone. She might laugh at something they said or something else, but I couldn't take my eyes off of her. She was mesmerizing. Eventually, I stopped resisting my need to have her all to myself.

I left my drink at an empty table and walked over to her. Her back was to me, so I tapped her on the shoulder.

"Hey." She smiled.

"Wanna get out of here? Go for a walk?"

When I asked Macy to go for a walk, I fully expected her to look for Patrick or tell me she needed to keep tabs on him, but instead, she smiled and nodded. We went back to our hotel room to get our coats and scarves so we could walk the grounds. The lodge boasted beautiful parks and walking paths, which I'm sure looked better when it wasn't covered in snow, but I really wanted to get Macy alone.

It was chilly outside. Both of us pulled our coats tighter.

"If you're too cold, we can always go back." Maybe I was an ass for bringing her out into the cold.

"I'm okay." She smiled and tucked her arm through mine.

For a while, we walked in silence, enjoying the beauty that lay all around us. The pristine snow blanketed everything. Normally, I would have wanted to have a snowball fight, run and jump in it, make snow angels, but it was so beautiful, I wanted it to remain untouched.

"So... Patrick? Will there be wedding bells anytime soon? You guys do look like one hell of a couple." I decided I wasn't going to beat around the bush about what happened this afternoon.

"So, you did hear her comment..." Macy pursed her lips and looked at me.

"Yeah... congratulations. It sounds like you're getting exactly what you want." I was brooding.

"Whoa. You're jumping the gun big time. Patrick is here with Celeste, and in case you've forgotten... I'm here with you. This isn't some movie where the maid of honor and best man run off together and leave their significant others stranded at the wedding."

We both laughed.

"Okay."

Relief flooded me. Macy still sounded a bit undecided. We fell into an easy silence for a moment. I decided to share something I'd been thinking about.

"You know this wedding has made me reflect on my own life. I think I might be ready to settle down."

Macy's steps halted. "Really? Somehow I thought you'd stay a bachelor forever."

I was puzzled. "Why would you think that?" I turned to her.

"Well... because you're a womanizer. You said you didn't want to settle down."

"Mace, I said that when we were in college. People say a lot of things when they're young... and I'm not a womanizer. Serial dater, yes. But how many serious girlfriends have you known me to have? And I've never cheated on anyone or tried to juggle women."

"Okay, but why now... what's changed?"

"I think I just needed to meet the right woman..."

The question was poised on her lips to ask who I was referring to, but she didn't ask. We stood on the path and stared into each other's eyes. I was ready to lean in and kiss her, but Macy broke whatever spell we found ourselves under.

She hugged herself, rubbing her hands up and down her arms. "I'm starting to get cold. Maybe we should head back inside... Plus, I'm sure Jennifer's looking for me."

I held her gaze. I swallowed down whatever I was going to say. "Okay... let's head back."

I would let her use all the excuses she wanted to put distance between us. I wasn't going to push her, but before this week was over, she would know how I felt, and she was either going to want to be in this with me... or... I wasn't sure where or would leave us. It felt like everything hung in the balance.

# CHAPTER 12

## Macy

Many people spent the day rehearsing for talent night, including many of the newly arrived guests. Coop said he had to deal with work, so I didn't see much of him.

Last night, as we'd gotten ready for bed, things had felt a bit tense. I was trying hard not to dive into why that was. I'd never really been someone that avoided dealing with things, but I knew there was a ten-ton elephant sitting in the room with Coop and I on a daily basis that I was trying not to deal with.

I ended up spending most of the day with Jennifer, going over things for the wedding day. When night finally fell, and it was time for the talent show. Coop still hadn't turned up and I wondered if everything was okay.

I took my seat in the front row and saved him a seat next to me.

Jennifer had made sure to tell me that Patrick was performing. I wondered briefly what he was going to do. When the lights dimmed, I looked around. Where was Coop? He was going to miss everything, and then we wouldn't be able to laugh about it all later tonight when we were back in our hotel room. The first act performed. One of the bridesmaids sung a song that sounded fitting for a beauty pageant. After her, a couple that had just arrived earlier that day did some kind of lounge act. Jennifer's uncle did a comedy routine. The next act that came up, was Patrick, and he wasn't alone. He and Celeste would be performing together.

I thought I would feel envious or upset, but I wasn't. I watched their duet and clapped right along with everyone else. Both of them had nice singing voices. Celeste waved to me before they left the stage and I waved back.

I kept wondering if Coop was ever going to show up.

A couple of performances later, I found out why he'd been missing all day when his name was announced. I sat forward in my seat. Was that a mistake? He was really going to perform? Days ago, I'd mentioned it and he'd brushed it off.

When the familiar intro to 'Swear It Again' by Westlife kicked in. I almost squealed and jumped out of my seat. Coop appeared on stage in some boy band attire and began singing the song.

In the car on the way here, he'd told me he didn't remember it. It was clear that was untrue. He sang every word perfectly and performed the dance routine he'd choreographed without a misstep. I was floored.

The whole time he sang, he kept his eyes glued to mine. Halfway through, I knew he was singing the song to me, and not just for nostalgia.

I couldn't help grinning like a fool as I watched him dance around the stage like he was in the Backstreet Boys.

We'd been friends for a long time, but Coop had really surprised me tonight.

The moment he finished, instead of walking offstage to wait with all the other participants, he came into the audience and pulled me to my feet.

He cupped my face in his hands and kissed me in front of everyone. This kiss was unlike the others he'd given me in public. I was so caught up in the moment, I kissed him back. His tongue swept into my mouth and it was like that night in my living room all over again.

When people starting yelling and whistling, the fog lifted, and I remembered we had an audience. Quickly, I pulled away. My face was flushed and heated. I was angry, but tried to mask it, when I grabbed Coop's hand and walked out of the ballroom.

Once the heavy door swung shut behind us, and I was sure we wouldn't be overheard, I folded my arms across my chest and turned to him. "What was that? No heavy PDA. That was a rule. I let the other kisses slide, because you didn't... you didn't..."

My emotions were in such disarray. I wasn't completely sure why I was so upset. This wasn't the first time that Coop had kissed me in public since we got here. It had been the first time he used tongue. Maybe I was upset because Coop seemed to know something that I couldn't or wouldn't face.

I ranted on and on about how angry I was over what he'd just done that I missed the signs that would have told me how angry, Coop was, so I was blindsided by his outburst.

"Maybe I'm sick of your rules." His face was flushed red.

"Have you ever thought that? Maybe that's why Patrick isn't interested now? Too many rules."

His words stung. I took a step back like he'd slapped me. The look on his face told me he regretted the words the minute he saw my reaction. It was clear he wished he could take them back, but they were already out there.

"Mace... I'm..."

I didn't give him the opportunity to apologize. I walked away without a backwards glance. Why is it always the people we care about that have the ability to wound us the deepest?

I wasn't sure where to go. I just didn't want to be around him or anyone, but an hour later, Coop found me down one of the corridors of meeting rooms that wasn't being used. I was huddled in the alcove of one of the entrances, only visible if you came down the hall.

The minute he spotted me, he sat down on the ground next to me. At first, he didn't say anything. We sat in silence.

"Mace... I'm so sorry for what I said. You know I love the person you are. I don't want you to change." Regret was palpable in every syllable.

Part of me wanted to hold onto my anger, because his words had hurt me. But when I looked at him, I knew it would hurt both of us more if I held a grudge. He was truly sorry.

"You're the last person I ever want to hurt... I hope you can forgive me." Again, his voice was swimming in remorse.

I nodded. "Yeah, I forgive you."

"Let's get out of this drafty hallway."

I let him take my hand and help me to my feet.

***

Later that night, in the bathroom, I fumbled with my head scarf.

Coop walked in behind me. "Here, let me do that." He'd already taken the fabric from me before I could protest. I knew he'd apologized, and I'd accepted, but it felt like he was still trying to make up for his asshole comments.

For a minute I peered at him over my shoulder, dumbfounded. "You know how to tie it?"

"Mace, we have known each other for the last sixteen years. I've had to listen to you talk about your natural hair. I've seen you do certain things to your hair often enough to know." Expertly, he tied the silk cloth on my head, taking care to make sure he tucked my hair beneath it. Despite the kisses we'd shared over the past few days. This by far felt like the most intimate thing he'd done for me.

Neither of us slept very well that night. Even though we'd had a reconciliation, something was still clearly amiss. The tossing and turning lasted most of the night.

***

Despite the restless night, I was up dressed and showered, before Coop woke up. It was the earliest I'd woken since we got here. Partly, because Jennifer had scheduled a breakfast for the bridal party. It was Christmas Eve and I should be giddy with excitement, like I always was during this time of year, but I wasn't.

Before I left the bedroom, I watched Coop sleep. Nothing creepy, it was only for a few seconds. I just wanted to see him, when he wasn't opening his mouth and messing something up. That wasn't fair. It wasn't something he did all the time. He actually usually said all the right things. The niggling thought that had been in the back of my mind since he uttered those words were what if he was right? What if my rules were just too much?

I headed down to the restaurant that was holding the breakfast. Jennifer had graciously saved me a seat next to Patrick. I wanted to throttle her. I knew she was well-meaning. She'd listened to me drone on for the last two months about Patrick, but then I show up to her wedding with Coop.

I kept a smile plastered to my face. I didn't want to rain my drama on Jennifer's big day. Patrick's leg or hand kept brushing up against my thigh under the table. The first few times I thought it was purely accidental. After the third time, I threw him a look. Celeste wasn't here. I didn't know what game he was playing at, but that's not how I got down.

Breakfast dragged on longer than I would have liked. The minute it finished I left the room quickly, trying to evade Patrick, but he caught me.

"Macy." He grabbed my arm, forcing me to turn around.

I looked from his hold on my arm to him.

"Sorry." He let me go. "I wanted to talk to you."

I folded my arms across my chest. "Talk."

Patrick looked around like we were conducting some sort of illegal business transaction. "Can we go someplace private?"

He must have thought I had boo-boo the fool written on my forehead. I would not be put in a compromising position. "We can talk right here."

I stared him down. Finally, he resigned himself to the fact that I wouldn't go anywhere private with him.

Patrick cleared his throat. "I wanted you to know that I've been doing some thinking... I think we should get back together."

My heart didn't flutter at his words.

"What about Celeste?" I narrowed my gaze, my eyes tiny slits, and peered at him like I was trying to see the man within.

"We were just having fun. She'll be fine. Seeing you here reminded me how good we were together. Everyone says so. You heard what the wedding coordinator said the other day. We're both attractive and successful. Think of all the things we could do together. We'd be a real power couple."

My stomach lurched. I was revolted, but before I could say anything someone called my name.

"Mace."

I turned around to find Coop standing there and he didn't look happy. How long had he been there? How much of what Patrick said had he heard?

Without addressing Coop, I turned back to Patrick. "You should go."

For a minute, he just stood there. He cut his eye at Coop before he said the next thing. "Think about what I said, okay."

I only nodded and let him leave. When I turned back to Coop, I wasn't sure what to say, where to begin. On unsteady legs, I approached him.

If I was still feeling the way about Patrick that I'd felt when we first got here, I might have asked Coop why he didn't stick to rule number two and make up an excuse to leave when he saw it was just Patrick and I in the hallway. But the rules no longer mattered, because I didn't care about Patrick anymore.

Now that my infatuation goggles had been removed, I'd finally been able to see Patrick for who he really was. I'd seen the smugness Coop tried to point out to me in the way Patrick assumed that I was just ready to jump back into a relationship. Nowhere in all the things he'd said had there been talk of love or passion. It had been about us making sense, looking good on paper. I didn't want that. I deserved better than to just be someone who fit the bill.

Now I stood in front of my best friend, and I knew my world wasn't finished falling down around me.

"What was that? I'm supposed to be your boyfriend." Coop's jaw ticked.

"But you're not." I said the words softly and without malice. "You're pretending... remember? We're pretending." Silence. "Coop... you are pretending, right?"

I asked the question, but I already knew the answer. This hadn't been a game for Coop. He'd come to claim my heart, but I was selfishly holding on to it.

# CHAPTER 13

## Cooper

"Maybe I don't want to pretend anymore, Mace." I sighed.

"I don't want to watch you with some other guy... I want to be the guy... I've been demonstrating that to you this whole time." Inside, it felt like someone was squeezing my heart.

"Coop... you're my best friend." Her voice trembled.

Was that all she would ever see me as?

"I want more Mace. I want all of you. I don't want to sit on the sidelines and hear about some other guy."

When she didn't say anything. I kept talking.

"I know you've been feeling something too or you wouldn't be resisting this so hard." I took her hand in mine.

"What if it doesn't work out and I lose my best friend?" The fear was so entrenched in her eyes and the stiffness of her body.

"But what if it does? Why do you have to see it as losing something? What if we're both gaining something? I'm scared too, but I'm willing to take a risk, to see if there is something there..." The only other time I'd been as vulnerable as I was right now was when Macy discovered my secret when we were thirteen. She'd held such power over me then. My life had been in her hands. There were so many other things she could have done or said that day to alter my existence. Right now, in this moment, she once again held my whole world in her hands.

"You're my home Mace... you've always been. Don't you understand."

Macy looked down at our hands. Tears gathered in her eyes.

"I don't think I can risk our friendship." She pulled her hand from mine. "I'm sorry."

I felt like someone had sucker punched me. So, this is what it's like when you're in love and it's not returned.

We stood there staring at one another, each of us wishing and willing the other would concede, come over to our side. She wanted to keep our friendship intact, but I needed her love, all or nothing.

When I realized she wasn't going to change her mind, I dropped my gaze to the floor. I took a deep breath.

"I can't stay." I finally looked at her again. It was one of the first times in my life I felt the sting of tears.

She wiped away a tear and I felt like shit for making her cry, but I was dying on the inside.

I bridged the divide between us and stepped into her personal space. Her smell, that mixture of coconut and fruit wafted up my nostrils. I wanted to inhale so I could keep it with me always. With shaking hands, I cupped her beautiful face, and kissed her one last time. I wasn't sure what this meant for us, but I needed her to know how I felt about her. I poured everything into the kiss, and then I walked away. Leaving her standing in the hallway. It was the hardest thing I'd ever done.

***

I didn't expect Macy to come back to the room before I left, because all of the bridesmaids were getting ready with the bride. I finished packing my things and left the Christmas gift I had for her on the bed.

Down in the lobby, I saw Patrick. Celeste was nowhere in sight and he was pacing the lobby in his tuxedo. Briefly I wondered if he was waiting to finish his conversation with Macy.

I needed to say something to that ass wipe before I left. I sat my bag down and approached him.

"Did Macy ever tell you how we met?" I leveled my menacing gaze at Patrick.

He halted and looked up startled. It took him a second, but he shook his head.

"It was in middle school. Seventh grade to be exact. Macy and her family had just moved to town. She was such a nerd..." Remembering the terrible way she used to dress made me chuckle. "She's still a nerd, just a really cool one, but I digress." I walked the few extra steps towards him with my hands in my pockets.

"They'd just moved to town and I thought she was an easy mark. You see, I was a bully. It wasn't just because. I wasn't just being an asshole because I could. I had to be one to survive... When you grow up always wondering where your next meal is coming from or having to protect yourself because you're sleeping on the streets, you learn real fast you're either going to be the predator or the prey... Poor Macy was my prey."

I would forever be sorry that I did that to her.

"After about a month of me terrorizing her and taking her lunch money, she followed me after school one day. When she realized I was homeless, I was sure she was going to narc on me or at least use the information to blackmail me, punish me or get me in trouble for all the things I'd done to her. I'd been horrible to her, I deserved it... it's what I would have done. I didn't expect any less from her..."

It wasn't often I reflected on that period in my life, but the memory was why I loved her so damn much, even if she didn't feel she could love me back the way I hoped she would. I would still continue to protect her.

"Do you know what she did instead? She invited me over for fucking dinner." I snorted. "Who does that?"

Patrick continued to stare at me. Clearly, too intimidated to speak, which was fine, it was a rhetorical question.

"I'd never met anyone that could still see the decency in people even after they'd done her wrong." I crossed my arms over my chest.

"After that day, she made sure no one ever found out about my secret and managed to help keep child services from carting me off to some crappy foster home. Hell, she even asked me once if I wanted her to get her parents to adopt me... Her family did take care of me. I had a place I could go to for meals when I needed to eat, and her mother would even take me shopping for school clothes."

I approached Patrick until I was nose-to-nose with that fucker. He flinched. It didn't go unnoticed that he thought twice about taking a step back. His pride was what kept him toe-to-toe with me.

"So, you see, that woman means the world to me... If she decides to take you back..." My nostrils flared at the thought. Unfortunately, Macy wanted him. What she saw in this jackass, I couldn't begin to fathom. While I wasn't going to stay here and watch her fall into his arms, I would make damn sure he didn't hurt her again.

"If she decides to take you back… and you hurt her, just know that I won't lay a hand on you." I held my fists up in front of his face, so he could see the scars that laced my knuckles from the fighting I had done over the years.

"Oh believe, I'll want to find you and give you a good ass whooping. I won't rule it out." The hard-piercing glare I delivered, let him know that I would certainly let things get physical if necessary.

"The thing is… I don't need to. Now, I'm a bully with a bank account and friends in high places." While maintaining eye contact, I reached up and straightened the lapels of his jacket.

"You hurt Mace…" My angry gaze roamed over his face. For a minute, my hold on his jacket tightened. "I'll make your life so fucking miserable, you'll wish you never met her."

Patrick's Adam's apple bobbed up and down. He knew I meant what I fucking said. I'd go all scorched earth on his ass if he caused one tear to fall from her eyes. Once more, I smoothed down the cheap fabric that I'd scrunched up in my fingers.

I gifted the bastard with a smile. "Enjoy the wedding and have a Merry Christmas." I gripped his shoulder in what some might have seen as a friendly gesture, but he knew the message I was sending him. I let him go, picked my bag up off the floor and walked away.

Outside the doors of the lodge, I didn't look back. There was a deep pain in the center of my chest, as I trudged to the parking lot. If I looked back, I might go to her again... and plead. My jaw tightened. I needed her to want me the way I wanted her. I wouldn't beg her. I put my bag in the trunk and climbed into the driver's seat of my SUV. When the engine rumbled to life, for a split-second I questioned if I was really leaving. With a steely resolve, I put the car into reverse and then pulled away.

In my rearview, I watched the lodge become smaller and smaller and I wondered if it would be the last time I saw Macy? I punched the steering wheel. Would the ache in my heart ever go away?

# CHAPTER 14

## Macy

After Coop left me standing in the hallway, I locked myself away in one of the public restrooms and cried my eyes out. Thank God for eye drops. I couldn't walk down the aisle with red, puffy eyes. I bought some from the store in the lobby before joining Jennifer and the other bridesmaids.

I was still reeling from my encounter with Coop. There was a good possibility, I'd just lost my best friend. He wanted more and I didn't want us to lose what we already had. I didn't want to lose his friendship I'd come to count on and depend on.

It was tough putting on a happy face for Jennifer when my head and my heart were in chaos, but I pushed through so I could be there for my friend.

I tried to find the tiniest bit of joy to cling to when I looked at the beautiful bridesmaid's gowns, I'd had a hand in picking out. The floor length pale pink gowns had a slit that came up to the thigh. The top of each gown was designed to be flattering for each individual bridesmaid. There were complimenting faux fur wraps to ward off the chill that we were sure to be feeling as we stood outside during the wedding. The gowns were lovely.

Once everyone, was in their dresses and make-up, we finished helping Jennifer with her final touches as the photographer shot the preparations from every angle.

Jennifer was a beautiful bride. Her lace wedding veil was fitted on her head and one of the other women handed her the bouquet. We all surrounded her, and stared into the floor length mirror with her, admiring her appearance. All I could feel was pain. I bit my quivering lip and smiled through it.

"Let's get you married. I know Kai is waiting for you at the end of that aisle."

Jennifer hugged me.

All of the bridesmaids filed out of the dressing room to get in line and be ready for the procession to begin.

I felt sick to my stomach when I looped my arm through Patrick's. I wouldn't look at him, although he tried to catch my attention more than once.

When the music started, I put one foot in front of the other and followed the person in front of me.

We all reached the end of the aisle and the groomsman filed off to the right to flank the groom, and the bridesmaids filed off to the left and waited for the bride. The music changed and Jennifer began her walk down the aisle.

Relief flooded me. I could finally let my tears flow and give myself the release I needed, knowing everyone would assume I was crying because of the wedding. I found myself looking out at the crowd, somehow hoping that Coop had changed his mind and stayed. No such luck.

I wasn't present, but I went through the motions. Took her bouquet when I needed to. Moved the train of her veil when it was necessary.

After the I do's, and the kiss, Jennifer and Kai were pronounced husband and wife. We went inside to take the pictures so everyone could warm up.

Once the pictures were completed, I had no luck avoiding Patrick. He cornered me so where we would be out of view.

"Did you think about what I said?"

No thought to the fact that as far as he was concerned, he'd probably broken Coop and I up. The selfish bastard only cared about himself. I was about to tell him about himself, when he leaned down and kissed me.

I felt nothing. My arms hung limply at my sides. Whatever I used to feel for Patrick was no longer there. The person I wanted more than anything was Coop, and he wasn't here, because of me.

When Patrick finally pulled away. I slapped him as hard as I could and walked away without saying a word.

Maybe Coop hadn't left yet, and I could fix this, fix what I had broken. Why had I been so afraid earlier to admit I had the same feelings? I wanted him too.

I knew Jennifer's reception was happening right now, but all I could think about was Coop. I chucked my bouquet, picked up my skirt and ran down the corridor and through the lobby until I reached the elevators. I was out of breath, but I didn't care.

The elevator was taking its sweet, precious time reaching the ground floor. I kept pressing the button, even though I knew that wouldn't make it come any faster.

Finally, the elevator arrived. I pushed the button for my floor, glad I was the only occupant. I wrung my hands while it slowly climbed upwards. When the doors opened, I burst onto our floor and ran down the hallway, nearly tripping in my haste to get to him.

Frantically, I swiped my key card in the door, hoping I hadn't missed him. The first few times the light kept flashing red.

"Damnit. Work already."

I took a deep, calming breath and swiped it once more. The green light glowed, and I pushed the door open.

"Coop? Coop are you here?" Hope clung to my words.

Fear gripped my heart. I rushed from the empty living room to the bedroom. Coop wasn't there, and his things were gone. The only thing left was a red velvet box that sat in the middle of the freshly made bed with a green bow on it. It must have been my Christmas gift. I sunk down onto the bed and took the case in my hands. I started to sniffle. I'd been an idiot.

With trembling fingers, I opened the lid. Nestled on top of the silk was a golden, heart-shaped locket. Tears sprang up in my eyes. I picked it up and opened it. On the left side was a picture of us as kids. I remembered the photo. It had been taken one of the first nights I got him to come to our house for dinner, after I'd discovered he was homeless. On the right-hand side was a recent picture of us taken at Thanksgiving by my mom.

If I was being honest with myself, the moment he kissed me in my apartment, things had changed. I'd been too stubborn, stupid and fearful to admit it. I loved my best friend. I was in love with him, and I may have lost him forever. I covered my hand with my mouth to hold back the sob. Why had I been so foolish? I'd gotten so caught up with trying to go after what I'd lost, and thought I wanted, that I hadn't let myself be open to something new. I'd let fear take the wheel and refused to see the possibility of a romantic relationship with Coop, the thought of there being an us. In doing so, I was the one who risked our friendship, not him. He was at least willing to try, because... because he loved me.

He hadn't said it out loud... but now I understood his actions. When you loved someone, you risked it all.

I held his locket in my hands ready to lay on the bed and weep, until I was in the right head space to make a plan on how I could get him back, when I heard someone jiggling the door handle and attempting to enter the room. I placed the box with the necklace on the nightstand and wondered if I needed to find a weapon.

Who was trying to get into the room?

# CHAPTER 15

## Cooper

"Mace... what are you doing here?" I stood in the open doorway.

For seconds, she just stared at me with her mouth hanging open.

"You're back." She said breathlessly.

I hadn't been expecting to find her here. Was it a good thing that she was here, or was I about to rehash the heartache all over again? My stomach dropped into my knees. I didn't walk any further into the room. I wanted to know what I was walking into, so if I needed to make a quick exit I could. "Yeah... I was nearly back in Chicago, and stopped to get gas and realized I must have left my wallet... I had to turn around and come back."

I held up my key card. "Forgot to turn it in, so I just came upstairs." I licked my lip. Shock coursed through me. Why was she here in the room? Wasn't the reception taking place right now? These same thoughts kept running in a circle inside my head. I wanted to ask but was afraid of being disappointed and getting my heart crushed all over again. *Man up.*

"What are you doing here?" I asked her again and held my breath.

Her big beautiful brown eyes had tears standing in them, but then her face lit up with the most radiant smile. Suddenly, she ran across the room and flung herself into my arms. I caught her and held onto her. What did this mean? I wanted to hope.

Her face was buried in my neck and she just held onto me. "I'm sorry."

My heart was beating an erratic rhythm. What was happening?

Macy pulled back to look at me. "Coop, it's you. I don't want Patrick. I want you. I'm sorry I was so stupid and stubborn..."

I silenced her with a kiss. Unlike the times before, Macy was very involved in this kiss. I heard a low moan in her throat.

I kicked the door closed with my foot and walked us into the bedroom. At some point we would need air, but I didn't want to stop kissing her, too afraid that I would wake up and realize I was dreaming.

She pulled away first.

"I want to see your dick." She gave me a huge grin and bit her lip. It made me whoop with laughter remembering the night I'd teased her. I'd wanted her bad.

"That I can do." I tossed her onto the bed and began to strip off my clothes.

Macy got onto her knees and pulled the shawl thingy draped on her shoulders, over her head. My mouth went dry and finally getting to see those perky round globes of hers. I toed off my shoes while she pulled her dress over her head.

She was now clad in only her bra and panties. I made quick work of my pants and shirt, until all I wore were my boxer briefs.

We both reached for each other at the same time. For a second, I expected it to be awkward because we'd been friends for so long, but it felt so right. Her skin was so soft beneath mine. We were greedy for each other, our kisses were hungry, and needy. It was like we were eating a meal but would never get full. Now that I had her, I'd never have enough of her.

I unclasped her bra and pulled it from her delectable body. I stepped back to admire her beauty. *Damn.* She was a beautiful woman.

"You're so fucking gorgeous."

I pulled her into my body and sucked her nipple into my mouth. Instantly, her fingers were in my hair, pulling and tugging. She was making purring noises that only made me want to keep doing what I was doing. I let her nipple go with a pop and sucked the other one into my mouth.

Soon that wasn't enough for either of us. I needed to be inside of her, but first I had to sample her. In my dreams I'd been thinking about tasting her all week.

I felt like I'd waited an eternity for this moment. I laid her on the bed and stood over her, looking at her sexy, toned body. Those legs. I hooked my fingers into the waist band of her panties and pulled them slowly down her long, shapely legs. Once she was naked, I couldn't stop licking my lips over her. I savored the sight of her plump pussy, damp with wetness. I couldn't wait to feast on her.

I crawled between her thighs my face parallel with those sweet lips. Seconds went by, and I couldn't tear my eyes away. It seemed like the more I stared the more she leaked. Finally, I dove in. I shut my eyes and licked her seam. Macy nearly came up off the bed. I placed my hand on the flat of her stomach to hold her in place. When I looked up at her from where I lay between her thighs, her head was thrown back, her lips parted.

Immediately, I went back to exploring her folds with my tongue. It wasn't long before her fingers were buried in my hair, gripping, pulling, pushing. She moaned her pleasure, and it was music to my ears to hear those sounds pour out of her.

I toyed with her, licking, nibbling, sucking her goodness until she was a writhing mess, beginning me to let her come. I knew I would never have enough of her.

When she finally came, she clutched the bed sheets in her fists, and screamed and moaned a bunch of incoherent nonsense. I loved every sound. The only thing I caught was my name. "Coop."

I smiled into her damp thigh before I kissed her quivering flesh and got up from the bed. My eyes were still trained on her delicious body as I pulled my underwear down and kicked them away.

Macy leaned up on her elbows and stared at my dick. It was standing straight up. I was so hard and ready to be inside of her.

I was about to step away and see if I had a condom, when Macy grabbed my hand. "I'm on the pill."

She tugged me down onto the bed. My lusty gaze raked her body. I climbed between her thighs and rubbed my dick along her wet folds. Macy cried out like she'd been scalded. If that was her response and I wasn't inside of her yet, I was eager to hear how vocal she could be.

I braced my arm next to her on the bed and stared her in the eyes as I began the slow slide inside of her.

She was so tight and warm. It was like being welcomed home.

When I was all the way inside of her, I stayed there. Letting her get used to the feel of me stretching her. The moment she wrapped those gorgeous legs of hers around me, I shut my eyes. I'd been dreaming of that moment for a while.

"Fuck me, Coop."

Those words falling from her lips were so damn sexy. I smiled down at her and pulled my dick out until only the tip remained inside and then I drove back into her.

She cried out and raked her nails down my back. I bit my lip and enjoyed the exquisite torture and sting of her scratching up my back, while she screamed out her pleasure.

I increased my pace. I didn't think either of us would last this first time. We were so hot for each other.

"Mace." I groaned out her name when she began to grind her pussy onto my dick every time, I pushed inside of her.

I reached between us and rubbed her clit, knowing it would drive her over the edge.

Macy screamed and came hard. Her nails dug into my back as her climax shook her body. I grunted and drove into her fast and deep before my own orgasm poured out of my body. I'd planned to pull out, but her legs were locked around me so tightly I couldn't. Pouring my seed into her, my flesh rubbing her walls, made my body tremble even more.

I was trying not to put all my body weight on top of her, but Macy was having none of it. She hugged me to her, kissing my neck. My lips grazed her jaw and then I cupped her face so I could kiss her full, plump lips, that were bee stung from my earlier kisses. We lay like that with me still inside of her, before my dick hardened minutes later, and I was ready for round two.

It was hours later by the time we were sated. She was snuggled into my chest, reeking of sex, and I wanted to lick every inch of her again.

Macy pulled away and sat up, her hair askew, skin glowing. "I got your gift. Will you put it on me?" She reached over to the nightstand and retrieved it.

I sat up and took the necklace from her. Macy turned so she was facing away from me. She lifted her hair out of the way so I could attach the clasp. Once it was on, she dropped her hair and turned to me.

"I love it... I love you." Her eyes glowed with the love she felt for me.

My heart melted at hearing those words fall from her lips. I'd held back earlier, because I didn't think it would be returned, and it had sacred the shit out of me to think about saying it and have her not say it back.

I reached for her. "I love you too, beautiful." When she pressed her lips to mine, I gave her the sweetest kiss. Something occurred to me. I pulled back and gave her a sly grin.

"By the way, I think you did forget your own name for a minute there. I think you were babbling." My laughter rang out after I teased her.

I told her I'd make her forget her own damn name, and I meant it.

Macy picked up a pillow and hit me with it, while she giggled.

I wrestled it from her and kissed her again, stealing her breath. It was safe to say that Christmas was going to find us right in this bed.

# EPILOGUE

## Macy

I snuck downstairs and into the kitchen, hoping to surprise Coop with breakfast in bed. I made the French toast he likes so much, bacon, eggs, a whole spread. I couldn't wait to wake him up. Hopefully, the smells wouldn't reach him upstairs before I could get up there with the food.

In my head, I pictured us eating in bed and maybe spending the whole day there. I grinned thinking about how we might spend the day. My parents and sister were expecting us, but we'd seen them last night.

Once I finished putting everything on a tray, I picked it up and carried it up the stairs, hoping again, he was still asleep.

With my foot, I pushed open the door and walked inside. When I saw Coop lying in bed with his arms behind his head, naked, except a red ribbon tied around his dick, I had to set the tray down before I dropped it. I was amused and aroused.

Giggling, I climbed into bed beside him. "I guess we both got a surprise this morning." I leaned down and kissed him. Coop placed his hand on the back of my head, deepened the kiss.

When he pulled away, I licked my lip.

"Do you like your gift?" Lust clouded his eyes.

I nodded. My gaze traveled down the length of his body until it came to rest on my gift. Under my gaze, he hardened even further.

"I figured we could spend the day trying out some positions we haven't done yet." I looked back up at him and when he reached for the Kama Sutra, the light glinted off of his gold wedding band. Seeing it made me smile, because it meant he was mine and I was his.

"I think my parents will understand if we don't make it over there. We are newlyweds after all." I moved closer and snuggled against him.

"Can you believe it's been a year?" He smoothed my hair away from my face.

I shook my head.

It had been a year since Coop declared he loved me, and I finally stopped being scared and admitted I loved him too. Yesterday, on Christmas Eve, we were wed in a small ceremony. It was the happiest day of my life.

I went to kiss him again, ready for him to make love to me.

"What about breakfast?"

We both looked at the tray of food. When I looked back at him, I grinned. "We can always warm it up later. Right now, I'm hungry for something else."

"Whatever you want Mrs. Brayden." He grinned.

"Merry Christmas, Coop."

"Merry Christmas, beautiful."

# A Very Alpha Christmas

https://ilovediverseromance.com/
a-very-alpha-christmas

# Acknowledgments

First and foremost, I always acknowledge and thank God for being able to do what I love. Without Him, none of this would be possible. Thanks to Sarah Kil for the awesome cover. This was my first time writing a friends to lovers romance. I hope I did Cooper and Macy justice.

I'm always super appreciative of the incredible support and encouragement I receive from my family and friends. A huge thank you and I love you to each of you. A huge shout out to all the awesome readers that read this book. I hope you enjoyed it. I'm tremendously grateful for all of you, for the new readers that may be reading my work for the first time, and for the loyal fans that pick up my books time and again. Thank you.

# What Did You Think of All I Want For Christmas Is An Alpha?

*First of all, thank you for purchasing this book **All I Want For Christmas Is An Alpha.** I know you could have picked any number of books to read, but you picked this book and for that I am extremely grateful.*

*I hope that it added value and quality to your everyday life. If so, it would be really nice if you could share this book with your friends and family by posting to Facebook and Twitter.*

*If you enjoyed this book and found some benefit in reading this, I'd like to hear from you and hope that you could take some time to post a review. Your feedback and support will help me as an author to greatly improve my writing craft for future projects and make this book even better.*

*I want you, the reader, to know that your review is very important and so, if you'd like to **leave a review,** all you have to do is go to Amazon, Goodreads or Bookbub and to do so. I wish you all the best in your future success!*

# *Spotify Playlist*

*I like to create soundtracks for my books.*
*Here's the soundtrack for*
*All I Want For Christmas Is An Alpha.*
*Listen to the playlist on my website, in the Extras section.*

You're My Best Friend – Queen

Have Yourself A Merry Little Christmas
– Sam Smith

All I Want For Christmas Is You – Mariah Carey

The Trouble With Love Is – Kelly Clarkson

Swear It Again - Westlife

White Christmas – Otis Redding

All I Want (For Christmas) – Liam Payne

That's What Love Can Do – Robin Thicke

Best Part (feat. Daniel Caesar) – H.E.R.

# Also By

# Stay Connected

Website:

https://moniboyce.com

Amazon:

https://www.amazon.com/author/moniboyce

Bookbub:

https://www.bookbub.com/authors/moni-boyce

FB Group:

https://www.facebook.com/groups/monismob

Goodreads:

https://www.goodreads.com/moniboyce

Facebook:

https://www.facebook.com/MoniBoyceWrites

Twitter:

https://www.twitter.com/moniboyce

Instagram:

https://www.instagram.com/moniboyce

Pinterest:

https://www.pinterest.com/moniboyce

Book + Main Bites:

https://www.bookandmainbites.com/moniboyce

Radish:

https://radishfiction.com/users/MoniBoyce

**To join newsletter, click on banner at the top of the page on my website.

# About the Author

Moni Boyce is an award-winning author of contemporary and paranormal romance, a filmmaker and a poet. After working in the film industry for fifteen years, helping others bring their visions to life, she now creates characters and worlds of her own. She considers herself a bookworm, film buff, foodie, music lover and an avid world traveler having visited 33 countries and counting. She currently lives in Virginia but considers Los Angeles her hometown.